Edgar Wallace was born illegitima[t] adopted by George Freeman, a porte eleven, Wallace sold newspapers at 1 school took a job with a printer. He enlisted in the Royal West Kent Regiment, later transferring to the Medical Staff Corps, and was sent to South Africa. In 1898 he published a collection of poems called *The Mission that Failed*, left the army and became a correspondent for Reuters.

Wallace became the South African war correspondent for *The Daily Mail*. His articles were later published as *Unofficial Dispatches* and his outspokenness infuriated Kitchener, who banned him as a war correspondent until the First World War. He edited the *Rand Daily Mail*, but gambled disastrously on the South African Stock Market, returning to England to report on crimes and hanging trials. He became editor of *The Evening News*, then in 1905 founded the Tallis Press, publishing *Smithy*, a collection of soldier stories, and *Four Just Men*. At various times he worked on *The Standard*, *The Star*, *The Week-End Racing Supplement* and *The Story Journal*.

In 1917 he became a Special Constable at Lincoln's Inn and also a special interrogator for the War Office. His first marriage to Ivy Caldecott, daughter of a missionary, had ended in divorce and he married his much younger secretary, Violet King.

The Daily Mail sent Wallace to investigate atrocities in the Belgian Congo, a trip that provided material for his *Sanders of the River* books. In 1923 he became Chairman of the Press Club and in 1931 stood as a Liberal candidate at Blackpool. On being offered a scriptwriting contract at RKO, Wallace went to Hollywood. He died in 1932, on his way to work on the screenplay for *King Kong*.

BY THE SAME AUTHOR
ALL PUBLISHED BY HOUSE OF STRATUS

The Clue of the
Twisted Candle

HOUSE OF
STRATUS

This edition published in 2001 by House of Stratus, an imprint of
Stratus Books Ltd., Lisandra House, Fore Street,
Looe, Cornwall, PL13 1AD, U.K.

www.houseofstratus.com

Typeset, printed and bound by House of Stratus.

A catalogue record for this book is available from the British Library
and the Library of Congress.

ISBN 1-84232-668-6

We would like to thank the Edgar Wallace Society for all the support they have given
House of Stratus. Enquiries on how to join the Edgar Wallace Society should be addressed to:
The Edgar Wallace Society, c/o Penny Wyrd, 84 Ridgefield Road, Oxford, OX4 3DA.
Email: info@edgarwallace.org Web: http://www.edgarwallace.org/

1

The 4.15 from Victoria to Lewes had been held up at Three Bridges in consequence of a derailment, and though John Lexman was fortunate enough to catch a belated connection to Beston Tracey, the wagonette which was the sole communication between the village and the outside world had gone.

"If you can wait half an hour, Mr Lexman," said the stationmaster, "I will telephone up to the village and get Briggs to come down for you."

John Lexman looked out upon the dripping landscape and shrugged his shoulders.

"I'll walk," he said shortly, and, leaving his bag in the stationmaster's care, and buttoning his mackintosh to his chin, he stepped forth resolutely into the rain to negotiate the two miles which separated the tiny railway station from Little Beston.

The downpour was incessant and likely to last through the night. The high hedges on either side of the narrow road were so many leafy cascades, the road itself was in places ankle deep in mud. He stopped under the protecting cover of a big tree to fill and light his pipe, and with its bowl turned downwards continued his walk. But for the driving rain which searched every crevice and found every chink in his waterproof armour, he preferred, indeed welcomed, the walk.

The road from Beston Tracey to Little Beston was associated in his mind with some of the finest situations in his novels. It was on this road that he had conceived *The Tilbury Mystery*. Between the station and the house he had woven the plot which made *Gregory Standish* the most popular detective story of the year. For John Lexman was a maker of cunning plots.

If, in the literary world, he was regarded by superior persons as a writer of "shockers," he had a large and increasing public who were fascinated by the wholesome and thrilling stories he wrote, and who held on breathlessly to the skein of mystery until they came to the dénouement he had planned.

But no thought of books, or plots, or stories filled his troubled mind as he strode along the deserted road to Little Beston. He had had two interviews in London, one of which under ordinary circumstances would have filled him with joy. He had seen TX, and "TX" was T X Meredith, who would one day be Chief of the Criminal Investigation Department, and was now an Assistant Commissioner of Police engaged in the more delicate work of that department.

TX, in his erratic, tempestuous way, had suggested the greatest idea for a plot that any author could desire. But it was not of TX he thought as he breasted the hill on the slope of which was the tiny habitation known by the somewhat magnificent title of Beston Priory.

It was the interview he had had with the Greek on the previous day which filled his mind, and John Lexman frowned as he recalled it. He opened the little wicket gate and went through the plantation to the house, doing his best to shake off the recollection of the remarkable and unedifying discussion he had had with the moneylender.

Beston Priory was little more than a cottage, though one of its walls was an indubitable relic of that establishment which a pious Howard had erected in the thirteenth century. A small and unpretentious building, built in the Elizabethan style with quaint gables and high chimneys, its latticed windows and sunken gardens, its rosary and its tiny meadow, gave it a certain manorial completeness which was a source of great pride to its owner.

He passed under the thatched porch, and stood for a moment in the broad hallway as he stripped his drenching mackintosh.

The hall was in darkness. Grace would probably be changing for dinner, and he decided that he would not disturb her in his present mood. He passed through the long passage which led to the big study at the back of the house. A fire burnt redly in the old-fashioned grate, and the snug comfort of the room brought a sense of ease and relief. He changed his shoes, and lit the table lamp.

The room was obviously a man's den. The leather-covered chairs, the big and well-filled bookcase which covered one wall of the room, the huge solid oak writing desk covered with books and half-finished manuscripts spoke unmistakably of its owner's occupation.

After he had changed his shoes he refilled his pipe, walked over to the fire, and stood looking down into its glowing heart.

He was a man a little above medium height, slimly built, with a breadth of shoulder which was suggestive of the athlete. He had, indeed, rowed "four" in his boat, and had fought his way into the semi-finals of the amateur boxing championship of England. His face was strong, lean, yet well-moulded. His eyes were grey and deep. His eyebrows straight and a little forbidding. The clean-shaven mouth was big and generous and the healthy tan of his cheek told of a life lived in the open air.

There was nothing of the recluse or the student in his appearance. He was in fact a typical healthy-looking Britisher, very much like any other man of his class whom one would meet in the mess-room of the British army, in the ward-rooms of the fleet, or in the far-off posts of the Empire where the administrative cogs of the great machine are to be seen at work.

There was a little tap at the door, and before he could say "Come in" it was pushed open and Grace Lexman entered.

If you described her as brave and sweet you might secure from that brief description both her manner and her charm. He half-crossed the room to meet her, and kissed her tenderly.

"I didn't know you were back until – " she said, linking her arm in his.

"Until you saw the horrible mess my mackintosh has made," he smiled. "I know your methods, Watson!"

She laughed, but became serious again.

"I am very glad you've come back. We have a visitor," she said.

He raised his eyebrows.

"A visitor? Whoever came down on a day like this?"

She looked at him a little strangely.

"Mr Kara," she said.

"Kara? How long has he been here?"

"He came at four."

There was nothing enthusiastic in her tone.

"I can't understand why you don't like old Kara," rallied her husband.

"There are very many reasons," she replied, a little curtly for her.

"Anyway," said John Lexman after a moment's thought, "his arrival is rather opportune. Where is he?"

"He is in the drawing-room."

The Priory drawing-room was a low-ceilinged rambling apartment, "all old print and chrysanthemums," to use Lexman's description. Cosy armchairs, a grand piano, an almost medieval open grate, faced with dull green tiles, a well-worn but cheerful carpet, and two big silver candelabra, were the principal features which attracted the newcomer.

There was in this room a harmony, a quiet order, and a soothing quality which made it a haven of rest to a literary man with jagged nerves. Two big bronze bowls were filled with violets, another blazed like a pale sun with primroses, and the early woodland flowers filled the room with a faint fragrance.

A man rose to his feet as John Lexman entered and crossed the room with an easy carriage. He was a man possessed of singular beauty of face and of figure. Half a head taller than the author, he carried himself with such grace as to conceal his height.

"I missed you in town," he said, "so I thought I'd run down on the off-chance of seeing you."

He spoke in the well-modulated tone of one who had had a long acquaintance with the public schools and universities of England. There was no trace of any foreign accent, yet Remington Kara was a

Greek, and had been born and partly educated in the more turbulent area of Albania.

The two men shook hands warmly.

"You'll stay to dinner?"

Kara glanced round with a smile at Grace Lexman. She sat uncomfortably upright, her hands loosely folded on her lap, her face devoid of encouragement.

"If Mrs Lexman doesn't object," said the Greek.

"I should be pleased if you would," she said almost mechanically; "it is a horrid night and you won't get anything worth eating this side of London, and I doubt very much," she smiled a little, "if the meal I can give you will be worthy of that description."

"What you can give me will be more than sufficient," he said, with a little bow, and turned to her husband.

In a few minutes they were deep in a discussion on books and places, and Grace seized the opportunity to make her escape. From books in general to Lexman's books in particular the conversation flowed.

"I've read every one of them, you know," said Kara.

John made a little face.

"Poor devil," he said sardonically.

"On the contrary," said Kara, "I am not to be pitied. There is a great criminal lost in you, Lexman."

"Thank you," said John.

"I am not being uncomplimentary, am I?" smiled the Greek. "I am merely referring to the ingenuity of your plots. Sometimes your books baffle and annoy me. If I cannot see the solution of your mysteries before the book is half through it angers me a little. Of course in the majority of cases I know the solution before I have reached the fifth chapter."

John looked at him in surprise and was somewhat piqued.

"I flatter myself it is impossible to tell how my stories will end until the last chapter," he said.

Kara nodded.

5

"That would be so in the case of the average reader, but you forget that I am a student. I follow every little thread of the clue which you leave exposed."

"You should meet TX," said John with a laugh, as he rose from his chair to poke the fire.

"TX?"

"TX Meredith. He is the most ingenious beggar you could meet. We were at Caius together, and he is by way of being a great pal of mine. He is in the Criminal Investigation Department."

Kara nodded. There was the light of interest in his eyes and he would have pursued the discussion further, but at the moment dinner was announced.

It was not a particularly cheerful meal because Grace as usual did not join in the conversation, and it was left to Kara and to her husband to supply the deficiencies. She was experiencing a curious sense of depression, a premonition of evil which she could not define. Again and again in the course of the dinner she took her mind back to the events of the day to discover the reason for her uneasiness.

Usually when she adopted this method she came upon the trivial causes in which apprehension was born, but now she was puzzled to find that a solution was denied to her. Her letters of the morning had been pleasant, neither the house nor the servants had given her any trouble. She was well in herself, and though she knew John had a little money trouble since his unfortunate speculation in Roumanian gold shares, and she half suspected that he had had to borrow money to make good his losses, yet his prospects were so excellent and the success of his last book so promising that she, probably seeing with a clearer vision the unimportance of those money worries, was less concerned about the problem than he.

"You will have your coffee in the study, I suppose," said Grace, "and I know you'll excuse me, I have to see Mrs Chandler on the mundane subject of laundry."

She favoured Kara with a little nod as she left the room, and touched John's shoulder lightly with her hand in passing.

Kara's eyes followed her graceful figure until she was out of view, then:

"I want to see you, Kara," said John Lexman, "if you will give me five minutes."

"You can have five hours, if you like," said the other easily.

They went into the study together, the maid brought the coffee and liqueurs and placed them on a little table near the fire and disappeared.

For a time the conversation was general. Kara, who was a frank admirer of the comfort of the room and who lamented his own inability to secure with money the cosiness which John had obtained at little cost, went on a foraging expedition whilst his host applied himself to a proof which needed correcting.

"I suppose it is impossible for you to have electric light here," Kara asked.

"Quite," replied the other.

"Why?"

"I rather like the light of this lamp."

"It isn't the lamp," drawled the Greek, and made a little grimace. "I hate these candles."

He waved his hand to the mantelshelf where the six tall white waxen candles stood out from two wall sconces.

"Why on earth do you hate candles?" asked the other in surprise.

Kara made no reply for the moment but shrugged his shoulders. Presently he spoke.

"If you were ever tied down to a chair and by the side of that chair was a small keg of black powder, and stuck in that powder was a small candle which burnt lower and lower every minute – my God!"

John was amazed to see the perspiration stand upon the forehead of his guest.

"That sounds thrilling," he said.

The Greek wiped his forehead with a silk handkerchief and his hand shook a little.

"It was something more than thrilling," he said.

"And when did this occur?" asked the author curiously.

"In Albania," replied the other. "It was many years ago, but the devils are always sending me reminders of the fact."

He did not attempt to explain who the devils were or under what circumstances he was brought to this unhappy pass, but changed the subject definitely.

Sauntering round the cosy room, he followed the bookshelf which filled one wall and stopped now and again to examine some title. Presently he drew forth a stout volume.

"*Wild Brazil*," he read, "by George Gathercole – do you know Gathercole?"

John was filling his pipe from a big blue jar on his desk and nodded.

"Met him once – a taciturn devil. Very short of speech and, like all men who have seen and done things, less inclined to talk about himself than any man I know."

Kara looked at the book with a thoughtful pucker of brow and turned the leaves idly.

"I've never seen him," he said as he replaced the book, "yet in a sense his new journey is on my behalf."

The other man looked up.

"On your behalf?"

"Yes – you know he has gone to Patagonia for me. He believes there is gold there – you will learn as much from his book on the mountain systems of South America. I was interested in his theories and corresponded with him. As a result of that correspondence he undertook to make a geological survey for me. I sent him money for his expenses, and he went off."

"You never saw him?" asked John Lexman, surprised.

Kara shook his head.

"That was not – " began his host.

"Not like me, you were going to say. Frankly, it was not, but then I realised that he was an unusual kind of man. I invited him to dine with me before he left London, and in reply received a wire from Southampton intimating that he was already on his way."

Lexman nodded.

"It must be an awfully interesting kind of life," he said. "I suppose he will be away for quite a long time?"

"Three years," said Kara, continuing his examination of the bookshelf.

"I envy those fellows who run round the world writing books," said John, puffing reflectively at his pipe. "They have all the best of it."

Kara turned. He stood immediately behind the author, and the other could not see his face. There was, however, in his voice an unusual earnestness, and an unusual quiet vehemence.

"What have you to complain about?" he asked with that little drawl of his. "You have your own creative work – the most fascinating branch of labour that comes to a man. He, poor beggar, is bound to actualities. You have the full range of all the worlds which your imagination gives to you. You can create men and destroy them. Call into existence fascinating problems, mystify and baffle ten or twenty thousand people, and then at a word elucidate your mystery."

John laughed.

"There is something in that," he said.

"As for the rest of your life," Kara went on in a lower voice, "I think you have that which makes life worth living – an incomparable wife."

Lexman swung round in his chair and met the other's gaze, and there was something in the set of the other's handsome face which took his breath away.

"I do not see – " he began.

Kara smiled.

"That was an impertinence, wasn't it?" he said banteringly.

"But then you mustn't forget, my dear man, that I was very anxious to marry your wife. I don't suppose it is a secret. And when I lost her I had ideas about you which are not pleasant to recall."

He had recovered his self-possession, and had continued his aimless stroll about the room.

9

"You must remember I am a Greek, and the modern Greek is no philosopher. You must remember, too, that I am a petted child of fortune, and have had everything I wanted since I was a baby."

"You are a fortunate devil," said the other, turning back to his desk and taking up his pen.

For a moment Kara did not speak, then he made as though he would say something, checked himself, and laughed.

"I wonder if I am," he said.

And now he spoke with a sudden energy.

"What is this trouble you are having with Vassalaro?"

John rose from his chair and walked over to the fire, stood gazing down into its depths, his legs wide apart, his hands clasped behind him, and Kara took his attitude to supply an answer to the question.

"I warned you against Vassalaro," he said, stooping by the other's side to light his cigar with a spill of paper. "My dear Lexman, my fellow countrymen are unpleasant people to deal with in certain moods."

"He was so obliging at first," said Lexman, half to himself.

"And now he is so disobliging," drawled Kara. "That is a way which moneylenders have, my dear man; you were foolish to go to him at all. I could have lent you the money."

"There were reasons why I should not borrow money from you," said John quietly, "and I think you yourself have supplied the principal reason when you told me just now, what I already knew, that you wanted to marry Grace."

"How much is the amount?" asked Kara, examining his well manicured fingernails.

"Two thousand five hundred pounds," replied John, with a short laugh, "and I haven't two thousand five hundred shillings at this moment."

"Will he wait?"

John Lexman shrugged his shoulders.

"Look here, Kara," he said suddenly, "don't think I want to reproach you, but it was through you that I met Vassalaro, so that you know the kind of man he is."

Kara nodded.

"Well, I can tell you he has been very unpleasant indeed," said John with a frown. "I had an interview with him yesterday in London, and it is clear that he is going to make a lot of trouble. I depended upon the success of my play in town giving me enough to pay him off, and I very foolishly made a lot of promises of repayment which I have been unable to keep."

"I see," said Kara, and then, "Does Mrs Lexman know about this matter?"

"A little," said the other.

He paced restlessly up and down the room, his hands behind him and his chin upon his chest.

"Naturally I have not told her the worst, or how beastly unpleasant the man has been."

He stopped and turned.

"Do you know he threatened to kill me?" he asked.

Kara smiled.

"I can tell you it was no laughing matter," said the other angrily. "I nearly took the little whipper-snapper by the scruff of the neck and kicked him."

Kara dropped his hand on the other's arm.

"I am not laughing at you," he said. "I am laughing at the thought of Vassalaro threatening to kill anybody! He is the biggest coward in the world. What on earth induced him to take this drastic step?"

"He said he is being hard pushed for money," said the other moodily, "and it is possibly true. He was beside himself with anger and anxiety, otherwise I might have given the little blackguard the thrashing he deserved."

Kara, who had continued his stroll, came down the room and halted in front of the fireplace, looking at the young author with a paternal smile.

"You don't understand Vassalaro," he said. "I repeat he is the greatest coward in the world. You will probably discover he is full of fire-arms and threat of slaughter, but you have only to click a revolver at him to see him collapse. Have you a revolver, by the way?"

"Oh, nonsense," said the other roughly. "I cannot engage myself in that kind of melodrama."

"It is not nonsense," insisted the other. "When you are in Rome, et cetera, and when you have to deal with a low-class Greek, you must use methods which will at least impress him. If you thrash him he will never forgive you, and will probably stick a knife into you or your wife. If you meet his melodrama with melodrama, and at the psychological moment produce your revolver, you will secure the effect you require. Have you a revolver?"

John went to his desk, and pulling open a drawer, took out a small Browning.

"That is the extent of my armoury," he said. "It has never been fired, and was sent to me by an unknown admirer last Christmas."

"A curious Christmas present," said the other, examining the weapon.

"I suppose the mistaken donor imagined from my books that I lived in a veritable museum of revolvers, sword-sticks and noxious drugs," said Lexman, recovering some of his good humour. "It was accompanied by a card."

"Do you know how it works?" asked the other.

"I have never troubled very much about it," replied Lexman. "I know that it is loaded by slipping back the cover, but as my admirer did not send ammunition, I have never even practised with it."

There was a knock at the door.

"That is the post," explained John.

The maid had one letter on the salver, and the author took it up with a frown.

"From Vassalaro," he said, when the girl had left the room.

The Greek took the letter in his hand and examined it.

"He writes a vile fist," was his only comment as he handed it back to John.

He slit open the thin buff envelope and took out half-a-dozen sheets of yellow paper, only a single sheet of which was written upon. The letter was brief:

"I must see you tonight without fail," ran the scrawl. "Meet me at the cross roads between Beston Tracey and the Eastbourne Road. I shall be there at eleven o'clock, and if you want to preserve your life you had better bring me a substantial instalment."

It was signed "Vassalaro."

John read the letter aloud. "He must be mad to write a letter like that," he said. "I'll meet the little devil and teach him such a lesson in politeness as he is never likely to forget."

He handed the letter to the other and Kara read it in silence.

"Better take your revolver," he said as he handed it back.

John Lexman looked at his watch.

"I have an hour yet, but it will take me the best part of twenty minutes to reach the Eastbourne Road."

"Will you see him?" asked Kara in a tone of surprise.

"Certainly. I cannot have him coming up to the house and making a scene, and that is probably what the little beast will do."

"Will you pay him?" asked Kara softly.

John made no answer. There was probably £10 in the house, and a cheque which was due on the morrow would bring him another £30. He looked at the letter again. It was written on paper of an unusual texture. The surface was rough almost like blotting paper, and in some places the ink, absorbed by the porous surface, had run. The blank sheets had evidently been inserted by a man in so violent a hurry that he had not noticed the extravagance.

"I shall keep this letter," said John.

"I think you are well advised. Vassalaro probably does not know that he transgresses a law in writing threatening letters, and that should be a very strong weapon in your hand in certain eventualities."

There was a tiny safe in one corner of the study, and this John opened with a key which he took from his pocket. He pulled open one of the steel drawers, took out the papers which were in it, and put in their place the letter, pushed the drawer to, and locked it.

All the time Kara was watching him intently, as one who found more than an ordinary amount of interest in the novelty of the procedure.

He took his leave soon afterwards.

"I would like to come with you to your interesting meeting," he said, "but unfortunately I have business elsewhere. Let me enjoin you to take your revolver, and at the first sign of any bloodthirsty intention on the part of my admirable compatriot, produce it and click it once or twice; you won't have to do more."

Grace rose from the piano as Kara entered the little drawing-room and murmured a few conventional expressions of regret that the visitor's stay had been so short. That there was no sincerity in that regret Kara, for one, had no doubt. He was a man singularly free from illusions.

They stayed talking a little while.

"I will see if your chauffeur is asleep," said John, and went out of the room.

There was a little silence after he had gone.

"I don't think you are very glad to see me," said Kara. His frankness was a little embarrassing to the girl, and she flushed slightly.

"I am always glad to see you, Mr Kara, or any other of my husband's friends," she said steadily.

He inclined his head.

"To be a friend of your husband is something," he said, and then as if remembering something, "I wanted to take a book away with me – I wonder if your husband would mind my getting it."

"I will find it for you."

"Don't let me bother you," he protested, "I know my way."

Without waiting for her permission he left the girl with the unpleasant feeling that he was taking rather much for granted. He was gone less than a minute and returned with a book under his arm.

"I have not asked Lexman's permission to take it," he said, "but I am rather interested in the author. Oh, here you are." He turned to John, who came in at that moment. "Might I take this book on Mexico?" he asked. "I will return it in the morning."

They stood at the door, watching the tail light of the motor disappear down the drive, and returned in silence to the drawing-room.

"You look worried, dear," she said, laying her hand on his shoulder.

He smiled faintly.

"Is it the money?" she asked anxiously.

For a moment he was tempted to tell her of the letter. He stifled the temptation, realising that she would not consent to his going out if she knew the truth.

"It is nothing very much," he said. "I have to go down to Beston Tracey to meet the last train. I am expecting some proofs down."

He hated lying to her, and even an innocuous lie of this character was repugnant to him.

"I'm afraid you have had a dull evening," he said, "Kara was not very amusing."

She looked at him thoughtfully.

"He has not changed very much," she said slowly.

"He's a wonderfully handsome chap, isn't he?" he asked in a tone of admiration. "I can't understand what you ever saw in a fellow like me, when you had a man who was not only rich, but possibly the best-looking man in the world."

She shivered a little.

"I have seen a side of Mr Kara that is not particularly beautiful," she said. "Oh, John, I am afraid of that man!"

He looked at her in astonishment.

"Afraid?" he asked. "Good heavens, Grace, what a thing to say! Why I believe he'd do anything for you."

"That is exactly what I am afraid of," she said in a low voice.

She had a reason which she did not reveal. She had first met Remington Kara in Salonika two years before. She had been doing a tour through the Balkans with her father – it was the last of the tours which the famous archaeologist made – and had met the man who was fated to have such an influence upon her life at a dinner given by the American Consul.

Many were the stories which were told about this Greek with his Jove-like face, his handsome carriage, and his limitless wealth. It was said that his mother was an American lady who had been captured by Albanian brigands and was sold to one of the Albanian chiefs who fell in love with her, and for her sake became a Protestant. He had been educated at Yale and at Oxford, and was known to be the possessor of vast wealth, and was virtually king of a hill district forty miles out of Durazzo. Here he reigned supreme, occupying a beautiful house which he had had built by an Italian architect, and the fittings and appointments of which had been imported from the luxurious centres of the world.

In Albania they called him "Kara Rumo," which meant "The Black Roman," for no particular reason so far as any one could judge, for his skin was as fair as a Saxon's, and his close cropped curls were almost golden.

He had fallen in love with Grace Terrell. At first his intentions had amused her, and then there came a time when they frightened her, for the man's fire and passion had been unmistakable. She had made it plain to him that he could base no hopes upon her returning his love, and in a scene which she even now shuddered to recall he had revealed something of his wild and reckless nature. On the following day she did not see him, but two days later when returning through the Bazaar from a dance which had been given by the Governor-General her carriage was stopped, she was forcibly dragged from its interior, and her cries were stifled with a cloth impregnated by a scent of a peculiar aromatic sweetness. Her assailants were about to thrust her into another carriage, when a party of British blue jackets who had been on leave came upon the scene, and, without knowing the nationality of the girl, had rescued her.

In her heart of hearts she did not doubt Kara's complicity in this mediaeval attempt to gain a wife, but of this adventure she had told her husband nothing. Until her marriage she was constantly receiving valuable presents which she as constantly returned to the only address she knew – Kara's estate at Lemazo. A few months after her marriage she had learned through the newspapers that this "leader of Greek society" had purchased a big house near Cadogan Square, and then to her amazement and to her dismay Kara had scraped an acquaintance with her husband – even before the honeymoon was over.

His visits had been happily few, but the growing intimacy between John and this strange, undisciplined man had been a source of constant distress to her.

Should she, at this the eleventh hour, tell her husband all her fears and her suspicions?

She debated the point for some time. And never was she nearer taking him into her complete confidence than she was as he sat in the big armchair by the side of the piano, a little drawn of face, more than a little absorbed in his own meditations. Had he been less worried he might have spoken. As it was she turned the conversation to his last work, the big mystery story which, if it would not make his fortune, would mean a considerable increase to his income.

At a quarter to eleven he looked at his watch, and rose. She helped him on with his coat. He stood for some time irresolutely.

"Is there anything you have forgotten?" she asked.

Should he follow Kara's advice? he asked himself. In any circumstances it was not a pleasant thing to meet a ferocious little man who had threatened his life, and to meet him unarmed was tempting Providence. The whole thing was of course ridiculous, but it was ridiculous that he should have borrowed, and it was ridiculous that the borrowing should have been necessary, and yet he had speculated on the best of advice – it was Kara's advice!

The connection suddenly occurred to him, and yet Kara had not directly suggested that he should buy Roumanian gold shares, but had merely spoken glowingly of their prospects. He thought a moment, and then walked back slowly into the study, pulled open the drawer of his desk, took out the sinister little Browning, and slipped it into his pocket.

"I shan't be long dear," he said, and, kissing the girl, he strode into the darkness.

Kara sat back in the luxurious depths of his car, humming a little tune, as the driver picked his way cautiously over the uncertain road. The rain was still falling, and Kara had to rub the windows free of the mist which had gathered on them to discover where he was. From time to time he looked out as though he expected to see somebody, and then with a little smile he remembered that he had changed his original plan, and that he had fixed the waiting room of Lewes junction as his rendezvous.

Here it was that he found a little man, muffled up to his ears in a big top coat, standing before the dying fire. He started as Kara entered and at a signal followed him from the room.

The stranger was obviously not English. His face was sallow and peeked, his cheeks were hollow, and the beard he wore was irregular – almost unkempt.

Kara led the way to the end of the dark platform before he spoke.

"You have carried out my instructions?" he asked brusquely.

The language he spoke was Arabic, and the other answered him in that language.

"Everything that you have ordered has been done, effendi," he said humbly.

"You have a revolver?"

The man nodded and patted his pocket.

"Loaded?"

"Excellency," asked the other in surprise, "what is the use of a revolver if it not loaded?"

"You understand, you are not to shoot this man," said Kara. "You are merely to present the pistol. To make sure you had better unload it now."

Wonderingly the man obeyed, and clicked back the ejector.

"I will take the cartridges," said Kara, holding out his hand.

He slipped the little cylinders into his pocket, and after examining the weapon returned it to its owner.

"You will threaten him," he went on. "Present the revolver straight at his heart. You need do nothing else."

The man shuffled uneasily.

"I will do all you say, effendi," he said, "but – "

"There are no 'buts,' " replied the other harshly. "You are to carry out my instructions without any question. What will happen then you shall see. I shall be at hand. That I have a reason for this play be assured."

"But suppose he shoots," persisted the other uneasily.

"He will not shoot," said Kara easily. "Besides, his revolver is not loaded. Now you may go. You have a long walk before you. You know the way?"

The man nodded.

"I have been over it before," he said confidently.

Kara returned to the big limousine which had drawn up some distance from the station. He spoke a word or two to the chauffeur in Greek, and the man touched his hat.

2

Assistant Commissioner of Police TX Meredith did not occupy offices in New Scotland Yard. It is the peculiarity of public offices that they are planned with the idea of supplying the margin of space above all requirements, and that on their completion they are found wholly inadequate to house the various departments which mysteriously come into progress coincident with the building operations.

"TX," as he was known by the police forces of the world, had a big suite of offices in Whitehall. The house was an old one facing the Board of Trade, and the inscription on the ancient door told passers-by that this was the "Public Prosecutor, Special Branch."

The duties of TX were multifarious. People said of him – and, like most public gossip, this was probably untrue – that he was the head of the "illegal" department of Scotland Yard. If by chance you lost the keys of your safe, TX could supply you (so popular rumour ran) with a burglar who would open that safe in half an hour.

If there dwelt in England a notorious individual against whom the police could collect no scintilla of evidence to justify a prosecution, and if it was necessary for the good of the community that that person should be deported, it was TX who arrested the obnoxious person, hustled him into a cab, and did not loose his hold upon his victim until he had landed him on the indignant shores of an otherwise friendly Power.

It is very certain that when the Minister of a tiny Power which shall be nameless was suddenly recalled by his Government and brought to trial in his native land for putting into circulation spurious bonds, it was somebody from the department which TX controlled who burgled His Excellency's house, burst the locks from his safe, and secured the necessary incriminating evidence.

I say it is fairly certain, and here I am merely voicing the opinion of very knowledgeable people indeed: heads of public departments who speak behind their hands, mysterious under-secretaries of State, who discuss things in whispers in the remote corners of their club-rooms, and the more frank views of American correspondents who had no hesitation in putting those views into print for the benefit of their readers.

That TX had a more legitimate occupation we know, for it was that flippant man whose outrageous comment on the Home Office Administration is popularly supposed to have sent one Home Secretary to his grave, who traced the Deptford murderers through a labyrinth of perjury, and who brought to book Sir Julius Waglite, though he had covered his trail of defalcation through the balance-sheets of thirty-four companies.

On the night of 3rd March TX sat in his inner office interviewing a disconsolate inspector of metropolitan police, named Mansus.

In appearance TX conveyed the impression of extreme youth, for his face was almost boyish, and it was only when you looked at him closely and saw the little creases about his eyes, the set line of his straight mouth, that you guessed he was on the way to forty. In his early days he had been something of a poet, and had written a slight volume of *Woodland Lyrics*, the mention of which at this later stage was sufficient to make him feel violently unhappy.

In manner he was tactful but persistent, his language was at times marked by a violent extravagance, and he had had the distinction of having provoked, by certain correspondence which had seen the light, the comment of a former Home Secretary that "it was unfortunate that Mr Meredith did not take his position with the seriousness which was expected from a public official."

His language was, I say, under great provocation, violent and unusual. He had a trick of using words which never were on land or sea, and illustrating his instruction or his admonition with the quaintest phraseology.

Now he was tilted back in his office chair at an alarming angle, scowling at his distressed subordinate, who sat on the edge of a chair at the other side of his desk.

"But, TX," protested the Inspector, "there was nothing to be found."

It was the outrageous practice of Mr Meredith to insist upon his associates calling him by his initials, a practice which had earned disapproval in the highest quarters.

"Nothing to be found!" he repeated wrathfully. "Glorious Mike!"

He sat up with a suddenness which caused the police officer to start back in alarm.

"Listen," said TX, grasping an ivory paper-knife savagely in his hand and tapping his blotting-pad to emphasize his words. "You're a pie!"

"I'm a policeman," said the other patiently.

"A policeman!" exclaimed the exasperated TX. "You're worse than a pie, you're a slud! I'm afraid I shall never make a detective of you," and he shook his head sorrowfully at the smiling Mansus who had been in the police force when TX was a small boy at school. "You are neither wise nor wily, you combine the innocence of a war baby with the gubbiness of a country parson – you ought to be in the choir."

At this outrageous insult Mr Mansus was silent. What he might have said, or what further provocation he might have received, may be never known, for at that moment the Chief himself walked in.

The Chief of the Police in these days was a grey man, rather tired, with a hawk nose and deep eyes that glared under shaggy eyebrows, and he was a terror to all men of his department save to TX, who respected nothing on earth and very little elsewhere. He nodded curtly to Mansus.

"Well, TX," he said, "what have you discovered about our friend Kara?"

He turned from TX to the discomfited inspector.

"Very little," said TX. "I've had Mansus on the job."

"And you've found nothing, eh?" growled the Chief.

"He has found all that it is possible to find," said TX. "We do not perform miracles in this department, Sir George, nor can we pick up the threads of a case at five minutes' notice."

Sir George Haley grunted.

"Mansus has done his best," the other went on easily, "but it is rather absurd to talk about one's best when you know so little of what you want."

Sir George dropped heavily into the armchair, and stretched out his long thin legs.

"What I want," he said, looking up at the ceiling and putting his hands together, "is to discover something about one Remington Kara, a wealthy Greek who has taken a house in Cadogan Square, who has no particular position in London society and therefore has no reason for coming here, who openly expresses his detestation of the climate, who has a magnificent estate in some wild place in the Balkans, who is an excellent horseman, a magnificent shot, and a passable aviator."

TX nodded to Mansus and, with something of gratitude in his eyes, the inspector took his leave.

"Now Mansus has departed," said TX, setting himself on the edge of his desk, and selecting with great care a cigarette from the case he took from his pocket, "let me know something of the reason for this sudden interest in the great ones of the earth."

Sir George smiled grimly.

"I have the interest which is the interest of my department," he said. "That is to say, I want to know a great deal about abnormal people. We have had an application from him," he went on, "which is rather unusual. Apparently he is in fear of his life from some cause or other, and wants to know if he can have a private telephone connection between his house and the central office. We told him that he could always get the nearest police station on the phone, but that doesn't satisfy him. He has made bad friends with some gentlemen of his own country, who sooner or later, he thinks, will cut his throat."

TX nodded.

"All this I know," he said patiently. "If you will further unfold the secret dossier, Sir George, I am prepared to be thrilled."

"There is nothing thrilling about it," growled the older man, rising, "but I remember the Macedonian shooting case in South London and I don't want a repetition of that sort of thing. If people want to have blood feuds let them take them outside the metropolitan area."

"By all means," said TX, "let them. Personally, I don't care where they go. But if that is the extent of your information I can supplement it. He has had extensive alterations made to the house he bought in Cadogan Square; the room in which he lives is practically a safe."

Sir George raised his eyebrows.

"A safe?" he repeated.

TX nodded.

"A safe," he said. "Its walls are burglar proof, floor and roof are reinforced concrete, there is one door which in addition to its ordinary lock is closed by a sort of steel latch which he lets fall when he retires for the night and which he opens himself personally in the morning. The window is unreachable, there are no communicating doors, and altogether the room is planned to stand a siege."

The Chief Commissioner was interested.

"Any more?" he asked.

"Let me think," said TX, looking up at the ceiling. "Yes; the interior of his room is plainly furnished, there is a big fireplace, rather an ornate bed, a steel safe built into the wall and visible from its outer side to the policeman whose beat is in that neighbourhood."

"How do you know all this?" asked the Chief Commissioner.

"Because I've been in the room," said TX simply, "having, by an underhand trick, succeeded in gaining the misplaced confidence of Kara's housekeeper, who, by the way" – he turned round to his desk and scribbled a name on the blotting-pad – "will be discharged tomorrow and must be found a place."

"Is there any – er – ?" began the Chief.

"Funny business?" interrupted TX. "Not a bit. House and man are quite normal save for these eccentricities. He has announced his intention of spending three months of the year in England and nine months abroad. He is very rich, has no relations, and has a passion for power."

"Then he'll be hung," said the Chief, rising.

"I doubt it," said the other. "People with lots of money seldom get hung. You only get hung for wanting money."

"Then you're in some danger, TX," smiled the Chief, "for according to my account you're always more or less broke."

"A genial libel," said TX; "but talking about people being broke, I saw John Lexman today – you know him?"

The Chief Commissioner nodded.

"I've an idea he's rather hit for money. He was in that Roumanian gold swindle, and by his general gloom, which only comes to a man when he's in love (and he can't possibly be in love, since he's married) or when he's in debt, I fear that he is still feeling the effect of that rosy adventure."

A telephone bell in the corner of the room rang sharply, and TX picked up the receiver. He listened intently.

"A trunk call," he said over his shoulder to the departing commissioner; "it may be something interesting."

A little pause, then a hoarse voice spoke to him.

"Is that you, TX?"

"That's me," said the Assistant Commissioner shortly.

"It's John Lexman speaking."

"I shouldn't have recognised your voice," said TX. "What is wrong with you, John – can't you get your plot to went?"

"I want you to come down here at once," said the voice urgently, and even over the telephone TX recognised the distress. "I have shot a man – killed him!"

TX gasped.

"Good Lord," he said, "you *are* a silly ass!"

3

In the early hours of the morning a tragic little party was assembled in the study at Beston Priory. John Lexman, white and haggard, sat on the sofa with his wife by his side. Immediate authority, as represented by a village constable, was on duty in the passage outside, whilst TX, sitting at the table with a writing-pad and a pencil, was briefly noting the evidence.

The author had sketched the events of the day. He had described his interview with the moneylender the day before the arrival of the letter.

"You have the letter?" asked TX.

John Lexman nodded.

"I am glad of that," said the other with a sigh of relief; "that will save you from a great deal of unpleasantness, my poor old chap. Tell me what happened afterwards."

"I reached the village," said John Lexman, "and passed through it. There was nobody about; the rain was still falling very heavily, and, indeed, I didn't meet a single soul all the evening. I reached the place appointed about five minutes before time. It was the corner of Eastbourne Road on the station side, and there I found Vassalaro waiting. I was rather ashamed of myself at meeting him at all under these conditions, but I was very keen on his not coming to the house, for I was afraid it would upset Grace. What made it all the more ridiculous was this infernal pistol, which was in my pocket banging against my side with every step I took as though to nudge me to an understanding of my folly."

"Where did you meet Vassalaro?" asked TX.

"He was on the other side of the Eastbourne Road and crossed the road to meet me. At first he was very pleasant, though a little agitated, but afterwards he began to behave in a most extraordinary manner, as though he was lashing himself up into a fury which he didn't feel. I promised him a substantial amount on account, but he grew worse and worse, and then suddenly, before I realised what he was doing, he was brandishing a revolver in my face and uttering the most extraordinary threats. Then it was I remembered Kara's warning."

"Kara?" said TX quickly.

"A man I know and who was responsible for introducing me to Vassalaro. He is immensely wealthy."

"I see," said TX. "Go on."

"I remembered this warning," the other proceeded, "and I thought it worth while trying it out to see if it had any effect upon the little man. I pulled the pistol from my pocket and pointed it at him, but that only seemed to make it – And then I pressed the trigger.

"To my horror four shots exploded before I could recover sufficient self-possession to loosen my hold of the butt. He fell without a word. I dropped the revolver and knelt by his side. I could tell he was dangerously wounded and, indeed, I knew at that moment that nothing would save him. My pistol had been pointed in the region of his heart – "

He shuddered, dropping his face in his hands, and the girl by his side, encircling his shoulder with a protecting arm, murmured something in his ear. Presently he recovered.

"He wasn't quite dead; I heard him murmur something, but I wasn't able to distinguish what he said. I went straight to the village and told the constable, and had the body removed."

TX rose from the table and walked to the door and opened it.

"Come in, constable," he said, and when the man made his appearance: "I suppose you were very careful in removing this body, and you took everything which was lying about in the immediate vicinity?"

"Yes, sir," replied the man; "I took his hat and his walking stick, if that's what you mean."

"And the revolver?" asked TX.

The man shook his head.

"There warn't any revolver, sir, except the pistol which Mr Lexman had."

He fumbled in his pocket and pulled it out gingerly, and TX took it from him.

"I'll look after your prisoner; you go down to the village, get any help you can, and make a most careful search in the place where this man was killed, then bring me the revolver which you will discover. You'll probably find it in a ditch by the side of the road. I'll give a sovereign to the man who finds it."

The constable touched his hat and went out.

"It looks rather a weird case to me," said TX, as he came back to the table. "Can't you see the unusual features yourself, Lexman? It isn't unusual for you to owe money, and it isn't unusual for the usurer to demand the return of that money, but in this case he is asking for it before it was due, and further than that he was demanding it with threats. It is not the practice of the average moneylender to go after his clients with a loaded revolver. Another peculiar thing is that if he wished to blackmail you, that is to say, bring you into contempt in the eyes of your friends, why did he choose to meet you in a dark and unfrequented road, and not in your house, where the moral pressure would be greatest? Also, why did he write you a threatening letter, which would certainly bring him into the grip of the law and would have saved you a great deal of unpleasantness if he had decided upon taking action?"

He tapped his white teeth with the end of his pencil and then suddenly – "I think I'll see that letter," he said.

John Lexman rose from the sofa, crossed to the safe, unlocked it, and was unlocking the steel drawer in which he had placed the incriminating document. His hand was on the key when TX noticed the look of surprise on his face.

"What is it?" asked the detective suddenly.

"This drawer feels very hot," said John. He looked round as though to measure the distance between the safe and the fire.

TX laid his hand upon the front of the drawer. It was, indeed, warm.

"Open it," said TX; and Lexman turned the key and pulled the drawer open.

As he did so, the whole contents burst up in a quick blaze of flame. It died down immediately and left only a little coil of smoke that flowed from the safe into the room.

"Don't touch anything inside," said TX quickly.

He lifted the drawer carefully and placed it under the light. In the bottom was no more than a few crumpled white ashes and a blister of paint where the flame had caught the side.

"I see," said TX slowly.

He saw something more than that handful of ashes, he saw the deadly peril in which his friend was standing. Here was one half of the evidence in Lexman's favour gone – irredeemably.

"The letter was written on a paper which was specially prepared by a chemical process, which disintegrated the moment the paper was exposed to the air. Probably if you delayed putting the letter in the drawer another five minutes you would have seen it burn before your eyes. As it was, it was smouldering before you had turned the key of the box. The envelope?"

"Kara burnt it," said Lexman in a low voice, "I remember seeing him take it up from the table and throw it in the fire."

TX nodded.

"There remains the other half of the evidence," he said grimly, and when, an hour later, the village constable returned to report that, in spite of his most careful search, he had failed to discover the dead man's revolver, his anticipations were realised.

The next morning John Lexman was lodged in Lewes gaol on a charge of wilful murder.

A telegram brought Mansus from London to Beston Tracey, and TX received him in the library.

"I sent for you, Mansus, because I suffer from the illusion that you have more brains than most of the people in my department, and that's not saying much."

"I am very grateful to you, sir, for putting me right with the Commissioner," began Mansus, but TX stopped him.

"It is the duty of every head of a department," he said oracularly, "to shield the incompetence of his subordinates. It is only by the adoption of some such method that the decencies of public life can be observed. Now get down to this."

He gave a sketch of the case from start to finish in as brief a space of time as possible.

"The evidence against Mr Lexman is very heavy," he said. "He borrowed money from this man, and on the man's body was found particulars of the very promissory note which Lexman signed. Why he should have brought it with him I cannot say. Anyhow I doubt very much whether Mr Lexman will get a jury to accept his version. Our only chance is to find the Greek's revolver – I don't think there's any very great chance, but if we are to be successful we must make a search at once."

Before he went out he had an interview with Grace. The dark shadows under her eyes told of a sleepless night. She was unusually pale and surprisingly calm.

"I think there are one or two things I ought to tell you," she said as she led the way into the drawing-room, closing the door behind him.

"And they concern Mr Kara, I think," said TX.

She looked at him, startled.

"How did you know that?"

"I know nothing."

He hesitated on the brink of a flippant claim to omniscience, but, realising in time the agony she must be suffering, he checked his natural desire.

"I really know nothing," he continued; "but I guess a lot." And that was as near to the truth as you might expect TX to reach on the spur of the moment.

She started without preliminary.

"In the first place I must tell you that Mr Kara once asked me to marry him; and for reasons which I will give you, I am dreadfully afraid of him."

She described without reserve the meeting at Salonika and Kara's extravagant rage, and told of the attempt which had been made upon her.

"Does John know this?" asked TX.

She shook her head sadly.

"I wish I had told him now," she said. "Oh, how I wish I had." She wrung her hands in an ecstasy of sorrow and remorse.

TX looked at her sympathetically. Then he asked: "Did Mr Kara ever discuss your husband's financial position with you?"

"Never."

"How did John come to meet Vassalaro?"

"I can tell you that," she answered. "The first time we met Mr Kara in England was when we were staying at Babbacombe on a summer holiday – which was really a prolongation of our honeymoon. Mr Kara came to stay at the same hotel. I think Mr Vassalaro must have been there before; at any rate they knew one another, and after Kara's introduction to my husband the rest was easy.

"Can I do anything for John?" she asked piteously.

TX shook his head.

"So far as your story is concerned, I don't think you will advantage him by telling it," he said. "There is nothing whatever to connect Kara with this business, and you would only give your husband a great deal of pain. I'll do the best I can."

He held out his hand and she grasped it, and somehow at that moment there came to TX Meredith a new courage, a new faith and a greater determination than ever to solve this troublesome mystery.

He found Mansus waiting for him in a car outside, and in a few minutes they were at the scene of the tragedy. A curious little knot of spectators had gathered, looking with morbid interest at the place where the body had been found. There was a local policeman on duty, and to him was deputed the ungracious task of warning his fellow villagers to keep their distance. The ground had already been searched very carefully. The two roads crossed almost at right angles, and at the corner of the cross thus formed the hedges were broken, admitting to a field which had evidently been used as a pasture by an adjoining dairy farm. Some rough attempt had been made to close the gap with barbed wire; but it was possible to step over the drooping strands with little or no difficulty. It was to this gap that TX devoted his principal attention. All the fields had been carefully examined without result, the four drains which were merely the connecting pipes between ditches at the sides of the cross roads had been swept out, and only the broken hedge and its tangle of bushes behind offered any prospect of the new search being rewarded.

"Hullo!" said Mansus suddenly, and stooping down he picked up something from the ground.

TX took it in his hand.

It was unmistakably a revolver cartridge. He marked the spot where it had been found by jamming his walking-stick into the ground, and continued his search, but without success.

"I am afraid we shall find nothing more here," said TX after half-an-hour's further search. He stood with his chin in his hand, a frown on his face, thinking.

"Mansus," he said, "suppose there were three people here – Lexman, the moneylender, and a third witness. And suppose this third person for some reason unknown was interested in what took place between the two men, and he wanted to watch unobserved. Isn't it likely that if he, as I think, instigated the meeting, he would have chosen this place because this particular hedge gave him a chance of seeing without being seen?"

Mansus thought.

"He could have seen just as well from either of the other hedges with less chance of detection," he said, after a long pause.

TX grinned.

"You have the making of a brain," he said admiringly. "I agree with you. Always remember that, Mansus – that there was one occasion in your life when TX Meredith and you thought alike."

Mansus smiled a little feebly.

"Of course, from the point of view of the observer, this was the worst place possible; so whoever came here, if they did come here, dropping revolver bullets about, must have chosen the spot because it was get-at-able from another direction. Obviously he couldn't come down the road and climb in without attracting the attention of the Greek who was waiting for Mr Lexman. We may suppose that there is a gate farther along the road; we may suppose that he entered that gate, came along the field by the side of the hedge, and that somewhere between here and the gate he threw away his cigar."

"His cigar?" said Mansus in surprise.

"His cigar," repeated TX. "If he was alone he would keep his cigar alight until the very last moment."

"He might have thrown it into the road," said Mansus.

"Don't jibber," said TX, and led the way along the hedge. From where they stood they could see the gate which led on to the road about a hundred yards farther on. Within a dozen yards of that gate TX found what he had been searching for: a half-smoked cigar. It was sodden with rain, and he picked it up tenderly.

"A good cigar, if I am any judge," he said, "cut with a pocket cutter, and smoked through a holder."

They reached the gate and passed through. Here they were on the road again, and this TX followed until they reached another cross road, that to the left inclining southward to the main Eastbourne Road, and that to the westward looping back to the Lewes– Eastbourne railway. The rain had obliterated much that TX was looking for, but presently he found a faint indication of a car wheel.

"This is where she turned and backed," he said, and walked slowly to the road on the left, "and this is where she stood. There is the grease from her engine."

He stooped down and moved forward in the attitude of a Russian dancer. "And here are the wax matches which the chauffeur struck." He counted: "One, two, three, four, five, six; allow two for each cigarette on a boisterous night like last night, that makes three cigarettes. Here is a cigarette end, Mansus – Gold Flake brand," he said, as he examined it carefully. "And a Gold Flake brand smokes for twelve minutes in normal weather, but about eight minutes in gusty weather. The car was here for about twenty-four minutes – what do you think of that, Mansus?"

"A good bit of reasoning, TX," said the other calmly, "if it happens to be the car you're looking for."

"I am looking for any old car," said TX.

He found no other trace of car wheels, though he carefully followed up the little lane until it reached the main road. After that it was hopeless to search, because rain had fallen in the night and in the early hours of the morning. He drove his assistant to the railway station in time to catch the train at one o'clock to London.

"You will go straight to Cadogan Square and arrest the chauffeur of Mr Kara," he said.

"Upon what charge?" asked Mansus hurriedly.

When it came to the step which TX thought fit to take in pursuance of his duty Mansus was beyond surprise.

"You can charge him with anything you like," said TX with fine carelessness. "Probably something will occur to you on your way up to town. As a matter of fact the chauffeur has been called unexpectedly away to Greece and has probably left by this morning's train for the Continent. If that is so we can do nothing, because the boat will have left Dover and will have landed him at Boulogne; but if by any luck you get him, keep him busy until I get back."

TX himself was a busy man that day, and it was not until night was falling that he again turned to Beston Tracey to find a telegram waiting for him. He opened it and read: "Chauffeur's name Goole. Formerly waiter English Club, Constantinople. Left for East by early train this morning, his mother being ill."

"His mother ill," said TX contemptuously. "How very feeble – I should have thought Kara could have gone one better than that."

He was in John Lexman's study as the door opened and the maid announced "Mr Remington Kara."

4

TX folded the telegram very carefully and slipped it into his waistcoat pocket. He favoured the newcomer with a little bow, and taking upon himself the honours of the establishment, pushed a chair to his visitor.

"I think you know my name," said Kara easily. "I am a friend of poor Lexman's."

"So I am told," said TX, "but don't let your friendship for Lexman prevent your sitting down."

For a moment the Greek was nonplussed, and then with a little smile and bow, he seated himself by the writing-table. "I am very distressed at this happening," he went on, "and I am more distressed because I feel that as I introduced Lexman to this unfortunate man I am in a sense responsible."

"If I were you," said TX, leaning back in the chair and looking half questioningly and half earnestly into the face of the other, "I shouldn't let that fact keep me awake at night. Most people are murdered as a result of an introduction. The cases where people murder total strangers are singularly rare. That, I think, is due to the insularity of our national character."

Again the other was taken aback and puzzled by the flippancy of the man from whom he had expected at least the official manner.

"When did you see Mr Vassalaro last?" asked TX, pleasantly.

Kara raised his eyes as though considering.

"I think it must have been nearly a week ago."

"Think again," said TX.

For a second time the Greek started and again relaxed into a smile. "I am afraid – " he began.

"Don't worry about that," said TX, "but let me ask you this question. You were here last night when Mr Lexman received a letter. That he did receive a letter there is considerable evidence," he said, as he saw the other hesitate, "because we have the supporting statements of the servant and the postman."

"I was here," said the other deliberately, "and I was present when Mr Lexman received a letter."

TX nodded. "A letter written on some brownish paper and rather bulky," he suggested.

Again there was that momentary hesitation. "I would not swear to the colour of the paper or as to the bulk of the letter," he said.

"I should have thought you would," suggested TX; "because, you see, you burnt the envelope, and I presumed you would have noticed that."

"I have no recollection of burning any envelope," said the other easily.

"At any rate," TX went on, "when Mr Lexman read this letter out to you – "

"To which letter are you referring?" asked the other with a lift of his eyebrows.

"Mr Lexman received a threatening letter," repeated TX patiently, "which he read out to you, and which was addressed to him by Vassalaro. This letter was handed to you, and you also read it. Mr Lexman to your knowledge put the letter in his safe – in a steel drawer."

The other shook his head, smiling gently. "I am afraid you've made a great mistake," he said almost apologetically. "Though I have a recollection of his receiving a letter, I did not read it, nor was it read to me."

The eyes of TX narrowed to the very slits, and his voice became metallic and hard.

"And if I put you into the box, will you swear you did not see that letter, or read it, or have it read to you, and that you have no know-ledge whatever of such a letter been received by Mr Lexman?"

"Most certainly," said the other coolly.

"Would you swear that you have not seen Vassalaro for a week?"

"Certainly," smiled the Greek.

"That you did not, in fact, see him last night," persisted TX, "and interview him on the station platform at Lewes; and you did not, after leaving him, continue on your way to London, and then turn your car and return to the neighbourhood of Beston Tracey?"

The Greek was white to the lips, but not a muscle of his face moved.

"Will you also swear," continued TX inexorably, "that you did not stand at the corner of what is known as Mitre's Lot and re-enter a gate near to the side where your car was, and that you did not watch the whole tragedy?"

"I'd swear to that!" Kara's voice was strained and cracked.

"Would you also swear as to the hour of your arrival in London?"

"Somewhere in the region of ten or eleven," said the Greek.

TX smiled. "Would you swear that you did not go through Guildford at half-past twelve and pull up to replenish your petrol?"

The Greek had now recovered his self-possession and rose. "You are a very clever man, Mr Meredith – I think that is your name?"

"That is my name," said TX calmly; "there has been no need for me to change it as often as you have found the necessity."

He saw the fire blazing in the other's eyes and knew that his shot had gone home.

"I am afraid I must go," said Kara. "I came here intending to see Mrs Lexman, and I had no idea that I should meet a policeman."

"My dear Mr Kara," said TX, rising and lighting a cigarette, "you will go through life enduring that unhappy experience – "

"What do you mean?"

"Just what I say; you will always be expecting to meet one person, and meeting another; and unless you are very fortunate indeed, that other will always be a policeman."

His eyes twinkled, for he had recovered from the gust of anger which had swept through him.

"There are two pieces of evidence I require to save Mr Lexman from very serious trouble," he said; "the first of these is the letter which was burnt, as you know."

"Yes," said Kara.

TX leaned across the desk. "How did you know?" he snapped.

"Somebody told me, I don't know who it was."

"That's not true," replied TX. "Nobody knows except myself and Mrs Lexman."

"But my dear good fellow," said Kara, pulling on his gloves, "you have already asked me whether I didn't burn the letter."

"I said envelope," said TX with a little laugh.

"And you were going to say something about the other clue?"

"The other is the revolver," said TX.

"Mr Lexman's revolver?" drawled the Greek.

"That we have," said TX shortly. "What we want is the weapon which the Greek had when he threatened Mr Lexman."

"There I'm afraid I cannot help you."

Kara walked to the door and TX followed.

"I think I will see Mrs Lexman."

"I think not," said TX.

The other turned with a sneer.

"Have you arrested her, too?" he asked.

"Pull yourself together!" said TX coarsely.

He escorted Kara to his waiting limousine. "You have a new chauffeur tonight, I observe," he said.

Kara, towering with rage, stepped daintily into the car.

"If you are writing to the other, you might give him my love," said TX, "and make most tender inquiries after his mother. I particularly ask this."

Kara said nothing until the car was out of earshot, then he lay back on the down cushions and abandoned himself to a paroxysm of rage and blasphemy.

5

Six months later TX Meredith was laboriously tracing an elusive line which occurred on an ordnance map of Sussex when the Chief Commissioner announced himself.

Sir George described TX as the most wholesome corrective a public official could have, and never missed an opportunity of meeting his subordinate (as he said) for this reason.

"What are you doing there?" he growled.

"The lesson this morning," said TX without looking up, "is maps."

Sir George passed behind his assistant and looked over his shoulder.

"That is a very old map you have got there," he said.

"1876. It shows the course of a number of interesting little streams in this neighbourhood which have been lost sight of for one reason or the other by the gentleman who made the survey at a later period. I am perfectly sure that in one of these streams I shall find what I am seeking."

"You haven't given up hope, then, in regard to Lexman?"

"I shall never give up hope," said TX, "until I am dead, and possibly not then."

"Let me see — what did he get — fifteen years?"

"Fifteen years," repeated TX; "and a very fortunate man to escape with his life."

Sir George walked to the window and stared out on to the busy Whitehall.

"I am told you are quite friendly with Kara again."

TX made a noise which might be taken to indicate his assent to the statement.

"I suppose you know that gentleman has made a very heroic attempt to get you fired," he said.

"I shouldn't wonder," said TX. "I made as heroic an attempt to get him hanged, and one good turn deserves another. What did he do? Saw Ministers and people?"

"He did," said Sir George.

"He's a silly ass," responded TX.

"I can understand all that" – the Chief Commissioner turned round – "but what I cannot understand is your apology to him."

"There are so many things you don't understand, Sir George," said TX tartly, "that I despair of ever cataloguing them."

"You are an insolent cub," grumbled his Chief. "Come to lunch."

"Where will you take me?" asked TX cautiously.

"To my club."

"I'm sorry," said the other with elaborate politeness. "I have lunched once at your club. Need I say more?"

He smiled as he worked after his Chief had gone at the recollection of Kara's profound astonishment and the gratification he strove so desperately to disguise.

Kara was a vain man. Immensely conscious of his good looks, conscious of his wealth. He had behaved most handsomely, for not only had he accepted the apology, but he had left nothing undone to show his desire to create a good impression upon the man who had so grossly insulted him.

TX had accepted an invitation to stay a weekend at Kara's "little place in the country," and had found there assembled everything that the heart could desire in the way of fellowship – eminent politicians who might conceivably be of service to an ambitious young Assistant Commissioner of Police – beautiful ladies to interest and amuse him. Kara had even gone to the length of engaging a theatrical company to play *Sweet Lavender*, and for this purpose the big ballroom at Hever Court had been transformed into a theatre.

As he was undressing for bed that night TX remembered that he had mentioned to Kara that *Sweet Lavender* was his favourite play, and he realised that the entertainment was got up especially for his benefit.

In a score of other ways Kara had endeavoured to consolidate the friendship. He gave the young Commissioner advice about a railway company which was operating in Asia Minor, and the shares of which stood a little below par. TX thanked him for the advice, and did not take it, nor did he feel any regret when the shares rose £3 in as many weeks.

He had superintended the disposal of Beston Priory. He had the furniture removed to London, and had taken a flat for Grace Lexman.

She had a small income of her own, and this, added to the large royalties which came to her (as she was bitterly conscious) in increasing volume as the result of the publicity of the trial, placed her beyond fear of want.

"Fifteen years," murmured TX as he worked, and whistled.

There had been no hope for John Lexman from the start. He was in debt to the man he killed. His story of threatening letters was not substantiated. The revolver which he said had been flourished at him had never been found. Two people believed implicitly in the story, and a sympathetic Home Secretary had assured TX personally that if he could find the revolver and associate it with the murder, beyond any doubt John Lexman would be pardoned.

Every stream in the neighbourhood had been dragged. In one case a small river had been dammed, and the bed had been carefully dried and sifted, but there was no trace of the weapon; and TX had tried methods more effective and certainly less legal.

A mysterious electrician had called at 456, Cadogan Square, in Kara's absence, and he was armed with such indisputable authority that he was permitted to penetrate to Kara's private room, in order to examine certain fitments.

Kara, returning next day, thought no more of the matter when it was reported to him, until going to his safe that night he discovered that it had been opened and ransacked.

As it happened, most of Kara's valuable and confidential possessions were at the bank. In a fret of panic and at considerable cost he had the safe removed and another put in its place of such potency that the makers offered to indemnify him against any loss from burglary.

TX finished his work, washed his hands, and was drying them when Mansus came bursting into the room. It was not usual for Mansus to burst into anywhere. He was a slow, methodical, painstaking man, with a deliberate and an official manner.

"What's the matter?" asked TX quickly.

"We didn't search Vassalaro's lodgings," cried Mansus breathlessly. "It just occurred to me when I was coming over Westminster Bridge. I was on top of a bus – "

"Wake up!" said TX. "You're amongst friends, and cut all that 'bus' stuff out. Of course, we searched Vassalaro's lodgings!"

"No, we didn't, sir," said the other triumphantly. "He lived in Great James Street."

"He lived in the Adelphi," corrected TX.

"There were two places where he lived," said Mansus.

"When did you learn this?" asked his Chief, dropping his flippancy.

"This morning. I was on a bus coming across Westminster Bridge, and there were two men in front of me, and I heard the word 'Vassalaro,' and naturally I pricked up my ears."

"It was very unnatural, but proceed," said TX.

"One of the men – a very respectable person – said: 'That Vassalaro used to lodge in my place, and I've still got a lot of his things. What do you think I ought to do?' "

"And you said?" suggested the other.

"I nearly frightened his life out of him," said Mansus. "I said: 'I am a police officer and I want you to come along with me.' "

"And of course he shut up and would not say another word," said TX.

"That's true, sir," said Mansus, "but after a while I got him to talk. Vassalaro lived in Great James Street, 604, on the third floor. In fact, some of his furniture is there still. He had a good reason for keeping two addresses, by all accounts."

TX nodded wisely.

"What was her name?" he asked.

"He had a wife," said the other, "but she left him about four months before he was killed. He used the Adelphi address for business purposes, and apparently he slept two or three nights of the week at Great James Street. I have told the man to leave everything as it is, and that we will come round."

Ten minutes later the two officers were in the somewhat gloomy apartment which Vassalaro had occupied.

The landlord explained that most of the furniture was his, but that there were certain articles which were the property of the deceased man. He added, somewhat unnecessarily, that the late tenant owed him six months' rent.

The articles which had been the property of Vassalaro included a tin trunk, a small writing bureau, a secretaire bookcase, and a few clothes. The secretaire was locked, as was the writing bureau. The tin box, which had little or nothing of interest, was unfastened.

The other locks needed very little attention. Without any difficulty Mansus opened both. The leaf of the bureau, when let down, formed the desk, and piled up inside was a whole mass of letters opened and unopened, accounts, notebooks and all the paraphernalia which an untidy man collects.

Letter by letter TX went through the accumulation without finding anything to help him. But it seemed as though he were upon a vain search, for the closest scrutiny failed to discover anything which would help him towards the end which he had in view. Then his eye was attracted by a small tin case thrust into one of the oblong pigeon-holes at the back of the desk. This he pulled out and opened, and found a small wad of paper wrapped in tinfoil.

"Hello, hello!" said TX, and he was pardonably exhilarated.

6

A man stood in the speckless courtyard before the Governor's house at Dartmoor gaol. He wore the ugly livery of shame which marks the convict. His hair was clipped short, and there was two days' growth of beard upon his haggard face. Standing with his hands behind him, he waited for the moment when he would be ordered to his work.

John Lexman – AO 43 – looked up at the blue sky as he had looked so many times from the exercise yard, and wondered what the day would bring forth. A day to him was the beginning and the end of an eternity. He dare not let his mind dwell upon the long, aching years ahead. He dare not think of the woman he left or let his mind dwell upon the agony which she was enduring. He had disappeared from the world: the world he loved, and the world that knew him, and all that there was in life. All that was worth while had been crushed and obliterated into the granite of the Princetown quarries and its wide horizon shrunken by the gaunt moorland with its menacing tors.

New interests made up his existence. The quality of the food was one. The character of the book he would receive from the prison library another. The future meant Sunday Chapel. The present whatever task they found him. For the day he was to paint some doors and windows of an outlying cottage – a cottage occupied by a warder who for some reason on the day previous had spoken to him with a certain kindness and a certain respect, which was unusual.

"Face the wall," growled a voice, and mechanically he turned, his hands still behind him, and stood staring at the grey wall of the prison storehouse.

He heard the shuffling feet of the quarry gang, his ears caught the clink of the chains which bound them together. They were desperate men, peculiarly interesting to him, and he had watched their faces furtively in the early period of his imprisonment.

He had been sent to Dartmoor after spending three months in Wormwood Scrubs. Old hands had told him variously that he was fortunate or unlucky. It was usual to have twelve months at the Scrubs before testing the life of a convict establishment. He believed there was some talk of sending him to Parkhurst, and here he traced the influence which TX would exercise, for Parkhurst was a prisoner's paradise.

He heard his warder's voice behind him.

"Right turn, 43, quick march."

He walked ahead of the armed guard, through the great and gloomy gates of the prison, turned sharply to the right, and walked up the village street toward the moors; beyond the village of Princetown, and on the Tavistock Road were two or three cottages which had been lately taken by the prison staff, and it was to the decoration of one of these that AO 43 had been sent.

The house was as yet without a tenant.

A paper-hanger, under the charge of another warder, was waiting for the arrival of the painter. The two warders exchanged greetings, and the first went off, leaving the other in charge of both men.

For an hour they worked in silence under the eyes of the guard. Presently the warder went outside, and John Lexman had an opportunity of examining his fellow sufferer.

He was a man of twenty-four or twenty-five, lithe and alert. By no means bad-looking, he lacked that indefinable suggestion of animalism which distinguished the majority of the inhabitants at Dartmoor.

They waited until they heard the warder's step clear the passage, and until his iron-shod boots were trampling over the cobbled path which led from the door, through the tiny garden to the road, before the second man spoke.

"What are you in for?" he asked, in a low voice.

"Murder," said John Lexman laconically.

He had answered the question before, and had noticed with a little amusement the look of respect which came into the eyes of the questioner.

"What have you got?"

"Fifteen years," said the other.

"That means eleven years and nine months," said the first man. "You've never been here before, I suppose?"

"Hardly," said Lexman drily.

"I was here when I was a kid," confessed the paper-hanger. "I am going out next week."

John Lexman looked at him enviously. Had the man told him that he had inherited a great fortune and a greater title his envy would not have been as genuine.

Going out!

The drive in the brake to the station, the ride to London in creased but comfortable clothing, free as the air, at liberty to go to bed and rise when he liked, to choose his own dinner, to answer no call save the call of his conscience, to see – He checked himself.

"What are you in for?" he asked in self-defence.

"Conspiracy and fraud," said the other cheerfully. "I was put away by a woman after three of us had got clear with £12,000. Damn rough luck, wasn't it?"

John nodded.

It was curious, he thought, how sympathetic one grows with these exponents of crime. One naturally adopts their point of view and sees life through their distorted vision.

"I bet I'm not given away with the next lot," the prisoner went on. "I've got one of the biggest ideas I've ever had, and I've got a real good man to help me."

"How?" asked John in surprise.

The man jerked his head in the direction of the prison.

"Larry Green," he said briefly. "He's coming out next month, too, and we are all fixed up proper. We are going to get the pile and then we're off to South America, and you won't see us for dust."

Though he employed all the colloquialisms which were common, his tone was that of a man of education, and yet there was something in his address which told John as clearly as though the man had confessed as much, that he had never occupied any social position in life.

The warder's step on the stones outside reduced them to silence, Suddenly his voice came up the stairs.

"Forty-three," he called sharply, "I want you down here."

John took his paint-pot and brush and went clattering down the uncarpeted stairs.

"Where's the other man?" asked the warder in a low voice.

"He's upstairs in the back room."

The warder stepped out of the door and looked left and right. Coming up from Princetown was a big grey car.

"Put down your paint-pot," he said. His voice was shaking with excitement. "I am going upstairs. When that car comes abreast of the gate, ask no questions and jump into it. Get down into the bottom and pull a sack over you, and do not get up until the car stops."

The blood rushed to John Lexman's head, and he staggered.

"My God!" he whispered.

"Do as I tell you," hissed the warder.

Like an automaton John put down his brushes, and walked slowly to the gate. The grey car was crawling up the hill, and the face of the driver was half enveloped in a big rubber mask. Through the two great goggles John could see little to help him identify the man. As the machine came up to the gate, he leapt into the tonneau and sank instantly to the bottom. As he did so he felt the car leap forward underneath him. Now it was going fast, now faster, now it rocked and swayed as it gathered speed. He felt it sweeping down-hill and up-hill, and once he heard a hollow rumble as it crossed a wooden bridge.

He could not detect from his hiding-place in what direction they were going, but he gathered they had switched off to the left and were making for one of the wildest parts of the moor. Never once did he feel the car slacken its pace, until, with a grind of brakes, it stopped suddenly.

"Get out," said a voice.

John Lexman threw off the cover and leapt out, and as he did so the car turned and sped back the way it had come.

For a moment he thought he was alone, and looked round. Far away in the distance he saw the grey bulk of Princetown Gaol. It was an accident that he should see it, but it so happened that a ray of the sun fell athwart it and threw it into relief.

He was alone on the moors! Where could he go?

He turned at the sound of a voice.

He was standing on the slope of a small tor. At the foot there was a smooth stretch of greensward. It was on this stretch that the people of Dartmoor held their pony races in the summer months. There was no sign of horses, but only a great bat-like machine with outstretched pinions of taut white canvas, and by that machine a man clad from head to foot in brown overalls.

John stumbled down the slope. As he neared the machine he stopped and gasped.

"Kara," he said, and the brown man smiled.

"But, I do not understand. What are you going to do?" asked Lexman, when he had recovered from his surprise.

"I am going to take you to a place of safety," said the other.

"I have no reason to be grateful to you, as yet, Kara," breathed Lexman. "A word from you could have saved me."

"I could not lie, my dear Lexman. And honestly, I had forgotten the existence of the letter, if that is what you are referring to; but I am trying to do what I can for you, and for your wife."

"My wife?"

"She is waiting for you," said the other.

He turned his head, listening.

Across the moor came the dull sullen boom of a gun.

"You haven't time for argument. They have discovered your escape," he said. "Get in."

John clambered up into the frail body of the machine and Kara followed.

"This is a self-starter," he said, "one of the newest models of monoplanes."

He clicked over the lever, and with a roar the big three-bladed tractor screw spun.

The aeroplane moved forward with a jerk, ran with increasing gait for a hundred yards, and then suddenly the jerky progress ceased. The machine swayed gently from side to side; and, looking over, the passenger saw the ground recede beneath him.

Up, up they climbed in one long sweeping ascent, passing through drifting clouds till the machine soared like a bird above the blue sea.

John Lexman looked down. He saw the indentations of the coast and recognised the fringe of white houses that stood for Torquay; but in an incredibly short space of time all signs of the land were blotted out.

Talking was impossible. The roar of the engines defied penetration.

Kara was evidently a skilful pilot. From time to time he consulted the compass on the board before him, and changed his course ever so slightly. Presently he released one hand from the control column, and, scribbling on a little block of paper, which was inserted in a pocket at the side of the seat, he passed it back.

John Lexman read: "If you cannot swim, there is a lifebelt under your seat."

John nodded.

Kara was searching the sea for something, and presently he found it. Viewed at the height at which they flew it looked no more than a white speck in a great blue field, but presently the machine began to dip, falling at a terrific rate of speed, which took away the breath of the man who was hanging on with both hands to the dangerous seat behind.

He was deadly cold, but had hardly noticed the fact. It was all so incredible, so impossible. He expected to wake up; and wondered if the prison was also part of the dream.

Now he saw the point for which Kara was making.

A white steam yacht, long and narrow of beam, was steaming slowly westward. He could see the feathery wake in her rear, and as the aeroplane fell he had time to observe that a boat had been put off. Then with a jerk the monoplane flattened out and came like a skimming bird to the surface of the water; her engines stopped.

"We ought to be able to keep afloat for ten minutes," said Kara, "and by that time they will pick us up."

His voice was high and harsh in the almost painful silence which followed the stoppage of the engines.

In less than five minutes the boat had come alongside manned, as Lexman gathered from a glimpse of the crew, by Greeks. He scrambled aboard, and five minutes later he was standing on the white deck of the yacht, watching the disappearing tail of the monoplane. Kara was by his side.

"There goes fifteen hundred pounds," said the Greek with a smile; "add that to the two thousand I paid the warder, and you have a tidy sum – but some things are worth all the money in the world!"

7

TX came from Downing Street at eleven o'clock one night, and his heart was filled with joy and gratitude.

He swung his stick to the common danger of the public, but the policeman on point duty at the end of the street, who saw him, recognised and saluted him, did not think it fit to issue any official warning.

He ran up the stairs to his office, and found Mansus reading the evening paper.

"My poor, dumb beast," said TX, "I am afraid I have kept you waiting for a very long time, but tomorrow you and I will take a little journey to Devonshire. It will be good for you, Mansus – where did you get that ridiculous name, by the way?"

"M or N," replied Mansus laconically.

"I repeat that there is the dawn of an intellect in you," said TX offensively.

He became more serious as he took from a pocket inside his waistcoat a long blue envelope containing the paper which had cost him so much to secure.

"Finding the revolver was a master-stroke of yours, Mansus," he said, and he was in earnest as he spoke.

The man coloured with pleasure, for the subordinates of TX loved him, and a word of praise was almost equal to promotion. It was on the advice of Mansus that the road from London to Lewes had been carefully covered and such streams as passed beneath that road had been searched.

The revolver had been found after the third attempt between Gatwick and Horsley. Its identification was made easier by the fact that Vassalaro's name was engraved on the butt. It was rather an ornate affair, and in its earlier days had been silver plated. The handle was of mother-o'-pearl.

"Obviously the gift of one brigand to another," was TX's comment.

Armed with this, his task would have been fairly easy, but when to this evidence he added a rough draft of the threatening letter which he had found amongst Vassalaro's belongings, and which had evidently been taken down at dictation, since some of the words were misspelt and had been corrected by another hand, the case was complete.

But what clinched the matter was the finding of a wad of that peculiar chemical paper, a number of sheets of which TX had ignited for the information of the Chief Commissioner and the Home Secretary by simply exposing them for a few seconds to the light of an electric lamp.

Instantly it had filled the Home Secretary's office with a pungent and most disagreeable smoke, for which he was heartily cursed by his superiors. But it had rounded off the argument.

TX looked at his watch.

"I wonder if it is too late to see Mrs Lexman," he said.

"I don't think any hour would be too late," suggested Mansus.

"You shall come and chaperon me," said his superior.

But a disappointment awaited them. Mrs Lexman was not in; and neither the ringing at her electric bell nor vigorous applications to the knocker brought any response. The hall porter of the flats where she lived was under the impression that Mrs Lexman had gone out of town. She frequently went out on Saturdays and returned on the Monday, and, he thought, occasionally on Tuesdays.

It happened that this particular night was a Monday night; and TX was faced with a dilemma. The night porter, who had only the vaguest information on the subject, thought that the day porter might know more, and aroused him from his sleep.

Yes, Mrs Lexman had gone. She went on the Sunday, an unusual day to pay a weekend visit, and she had taken with her two bags. The porter ventured the opinion that she was rather excited, but when asked to define the symptoms relapsed into a chaos of incoherent "you-knows," and "what-I-means."

"I don't like this," said TX suddenly. "Does anybody know that we have made these discoveries?"

"Nobody outside the offices," said Mansus, "unless, unless – "

"Unless what?" asked the other irritably. "Don't be a jimp, Mansus. Get it off your mind. What is it?"

"I am wondering," said Mansus, slowly, "if the landlord at Great James Street said anything. He knows we have made a search."

"We can easily find that out," said TX.

They hailed a taxi and drove to Great James Street. That respectable thoroughfare was wrapped in sleep, and it was some time before the landlord could be aroused. Recognising TX, he checked his sarcasm, which he had prepared for a keyless lodger, and led the way into the drawing-room.

"You didn't tell me not to speak about it, Mr Meredith," he said, in an aggrieved tone, "and as a matter of fact I have spoke to nobody except the gentleman who called the same day."

"What did he want?" asked TX.

"He said he had only just discovered that Mr Vassalaro had stayed with me, and he wanted to pay whatever rent was due," replied the other.

"What sort of man was he?" asked TX.

The brief description the man gave sent a cold chill to the Commissioner's heart.

"Kara, for a ducat!" he said, and swore, long and variously.

"Cadogan Square," he ordered.

His ring was answered promptly. Mr Kara was out of town, had, indeed, been out of town since Saturday. This much the man-servant explained with a suspicious eye upon his visitors, remembering that his predecessor had lost his job from a too confiding friendliness with spurious electric fitters. He did not know when Mr Kara would

53

return, perhaps it would be a long time and perhaps a short time. He might come back that night or he might not.

"You are wasting your young life," said TX bitterly. "You ought to be a fortune-teller."

"This settles the matter," he said in the cab on the way back. "Find out the first train for Tavistock in the morning, and wire the George Hotel to have a car waiting."

"Why not go tonight?" suggested the other, "there is the midnight train. It is rather slow, but it will get you there by six or seven in the morning."

"Too late," he said, "unless you can invent a method of getting from here to Paddington in about fifty seconds."

The morning journey to Devonshire was a dispiriting one despite the fineness of the day. TX had an uncomfortable sense that something distressing had happened. The run across the moor in the fresh spring air revived him a little.

As they spun down to the valley of the Dart, Mansus touched his arm.

"Look at that," he said, and pointed to the blue heavens where, a mile above their heads, a white-winged aeroplane, looking no larger than a very distant dragonfly, shimmered in the sunlight.

"By Jove!" said TX. "What an excellent way for a man to escape!"

"It's about the only way," said Mansus.

The significance of the aeroplane was borne in upon TX a few minutes later when he was held up by an armed guard. A glance at his card was enough to pass him.

"What is the matter?" he asked.

"A prisoner has escaped," said the sentry.

"Escaped – by aeroplane?" asked TX.

"I don't know anything about aeroplanes, sir; all I know is that one of the working party got away."

The car came to the gates of the prison and TX sprang out, followed by his assistant. He had no difficulty in finding the Governor: a greatly perturbed man, for an escape is a very serious matter.

The official was inclined to be brusque in his manner, but again the magic card produced a soothing effect.

"I am rather rattled," said the Governor; "one of my men has got away. I suppose you know that?"

"And I am afraid another of your men is going away, sir," said TX, who had a curious reverence for military authority. He produced his paper and laid it on the Governor's table.

"This is an order for the release of John Lexman, convicted under sentence of fifteen years' penal servitude."

The Governor looked at it.

"Dated last night," he said, and breathed a long sigh of relief. "Thank the Lord! – that is the man who escaped!"

8

Two years after the events described in the last chapter, TX, journeying up to London from Bath, was attracted by a paragraph in the *Morning Post*. It told him briefly that Mr Remington Kara, the influential leader of the Greek Colony, had been the guest of honour at a dinner of the Hellenic Society.

TX had only seen Kara for a brief space of time following that tragic morning when he had discovered not only that his best friend had escaped from Dartmoor prison and disappeared as it were from the world at a moment when his pardon had been signed, but that that friend's wife had also vanished from the face of the earth.

At the same time, it might, as even TX admitted, have been the veriest coincidence that Kara had also cleared out of London to reappear at the end of six months. Any question addressed to him concerning the whereabouts of the two unhappy people was met with a bland expression of ignorance as to their whereabouts.

John Lexman was somewhere in the world, hiding as he believed from justice, and with him was his wife. TX had no doubt in his mind as to this solution of the puzzle. He had caused to be published the story of the pardon and the circumstances under which that pardon had been secured; and he had, moreover, arranged for an advertisement to be inserted in the principal papers of every European country.

It was a moot question amongst the departmental lawyers as to whether John Lexman was not guilty of a technical and punishable offence for prison breaking, but this possibility did not keep TX awake at nights. The circumstances of the escape had been carefully examined. The warder responsible had been discharged from the service, and had almost immediately purchased for himself a beer-house in Falmouth for a sum which left no doubt in the official mind that he had been the recipient of a heavy bribe.

Who had been the guiding spirit in that escape – Mrs Lexman, or Kara?

It was impossible to connect Kara with the event. The motor car had been traced to Exeter, where it had been hired by a "foreign-looking gentleman"; but the chauffeur, whoever he was, had made good his escape. An inspection of Kara's hangars at Wembley showed that his two monoplanes had not been removed, and TX failed entirely to trace the owner of the machine he had seen flying over Dartmoor on the fatal morning.

TX was somewhat baffled and a little amused by the disinclination of the authorities to believe that the escape had been effected by this method at all. All the events of the trial came back to him as he watched the landscape spinning past.

He put down the newspaper with a little sigh, put his feet on the cushions of the opposite seat, and gave himself up to reverie. Presently he returned to his journals and searched them idly for something to interest him in the final stretch of journey between Newbury and Paddington.

Presently he found it in a two-column article with the uninspiring title, "The Mineral Wealth of Tierra del Fuego." It was written brightly, with a style which was at once easy and informative. It told of adventures in the marshes behind St Sebastian Bay and journeys up the Guarez Celman river, of nights spent in primeval forests, and ended in a geological survey wherein the commercial value of syenite, porphyry, trachite, and dialite were severally canvassed.

The article was signed "G G." It was said of TX that his greatest virtue was his curiosity. He had at the tip of his fingers the names of all the big explorers and author-travellers, and for some reason he could not place "G G" to his satisfaction – in fact, he had an absurd desire to interpret the initials into "George Grossmith." His inability to identify the writer irritated him, and his first act on reaching his office was to telephone to one of the literary editors of *The Times* whom he knew.

"Not my department," was the chilly reply, "and besides, we never give away the names of our contributors. Speaking as a person outside the office I should say that 'G G' was 'George Gathercole' – the explorer, you know, the fellow who had an arm chewed off by a lion or something."

"George Gathercole!" repeated TX. "What an ass I am!"

"Yes," said the voice at the other end of the wire, and he had rung off before TX could think of something suitable to say.

Having elucidated this little side-line of mystery, the matter passed from the young Commissioner's mind. It happened that morning that his work consisted of dealing with John Lexman's estate.

With the disappearance of the couple he had taken over control of their belongings. It had not embarrassed him to discover that he was an executor under Lexman's will, for he had already acted as trustee to the wife's small estate, and had been one of the parties to the ante-nuptial contract which John Lexman had made before his marriage.

The estate revenues had increased very considerably. All the vanished author's books were selling as they had never sold before, and the executor's work was made the heavier by the fact that Grace Lexman had possessed an aunt who had most inconsiderately died, leaving a considerable fortune to her "unhappy niece."

"I will keep the trusteeship another year," he told the solicitor who came to consult him that morning. "At the end of that time I shall go to the court for relief."

"Do you think they will ever turn up?" asked the solicitor, an elderly and unimaginative man.

"Of course they'll turn up!" said TX impatiently; "all the heroes of Lexman's books turn up sooner or later. He will discover himself to us at a suitable moment, and we shall be properly thrilled."

That Lexman would return he was sure. It was a faith from which he did not swerve.

He had as implicit a confidence that one day or other Kara the magnificent would play into his hands.

There were some queer stories in circulation concerning the Greek, but on the whole they were stories and rumours which were difficult to separate from the malicious gossip which invariably attaches itself to the rich and to the successful.

One of these was that Kara desired something more than an Albanian chieftainship, which he undoubtedly enjoyed. There were whispers of wider and higher ambitions. Though his father had been born a Greek, he had indubitably descended in a direct line from one of those old Mprets of Albania who had exercised their brief authority over that turbulent land.

The man's passion was for power. To this end he did not spare himself. It was said that he utilised his vast wealth for this reason, and none other, and that whatever might have been the irregularities of his youth – and there were adduced concrete instances – he was seeking toward an end with a singleness of purpose from which it was difficult to withhold admiration.

TX kept in his locked desk a little red book, steel bound and triple locked, which he called his "Scandalaria." In this he inscribed in his own irregular writing the tit-bits which might not be published, and which often helped an investigator to light upon the missing threads of a problem. In truth, he scorned no source of information, and was wholly conscienceless in the compilation of this somewhat chaotic record.

The affairs of John Lexman recalled Kara and Kara's great reception. Mansus would have made arrangements to secure a verbatim report of the speeches which were made, and these would be in his hands by the night. Mansus did not tell him that Kara was financing some very influential people indeed, that a certain Under-Secretary of State with a great number of very influential relations had been saved from bankruptcy by the timely advances which M. Kara had made. This TX had obtained through sources which might be hastily described as discreditable. Mansus knew of the baccarat establishment in Albemarle Street, but he did not know that the neurotic wife of a very great man indeed, no less than the Minister of Justice, was a frequent visitor to that establishment, and that she had lost in one night some £6000.

It was all sordid but, unfortunately, conventional, because highly placed people will always do under-bred things where money or women are concerned, but it was necessary for the proper conduct of the department which TX directed that however sordid and however conventional might be the errors which the great ones of the earth committed, they should be filed for reference.

The motto which TX went upon in life was "You never know."

The Minister of Justice was a very important person, for he was a personal friend of half the monarchs of Europe. A poor man with two or three thousand a year of his own, with no very definite political views and uncommitted to the more violent policies of either party, he succeeded in serving both, with profit to himself, and without earning the obloquy of either. Though he did not pursue the blatant policy of the Vicar of Bray, yet it is a fact which may be confirmed from the reader's own knowledge that he served in four different administrations, drawing the pay and emoluments of his office from each, though the fundamental policies of those four Governments were distinct.

Lady Bartholomew, the wife of this adaptable Minister, had recently departed for San Remo. The newspapers announced the fact and spoke vaguely of a breakdown which prevented the lady from fulfilling her social engagements.

TX, ever a Doubting Thomas, could trace no visit of nerve specialist nor yet of the family practitioner to the official residence in Downing Street, and therefore he drew conclusions. In his own *Who's Who*, TX noted the hobbies of his victims, which, by the way, did not always coincide with the innocent occupations set against their names in the more pretentious volume. Their follies and their weaknesses found a place and were recorded at length (as it might seem to the uninformed observer) beyond the limit which charity allowed.

Lady Bartholomew's name appeared not once but many times in the erratic records which TX kept. There was a plain matter-of-fact and wholly unobjectionable statement that she was born in 1874, that she was the seventh daughter of the Earl of Balmorley, that she had one daughter who rejoiced in the somewhat unpromising name of

Belinda Mary, and such further information as a man might get without going to a great deal of trouble.

TX, refreshing his memory from the little red book, wondered what unexpected tragedy had sent Lady Bartholomew out of London in the middle of the season. The information was that the lady was fairly well off at this moment, and this fact made matters all the more puzzling, and almost induced him to believe that after all the story was true and a nervous breakdown really was the cause of her sudden departure. He sent for Mansus.

"You saw Lady Bartholomew off at Charing Cross, I suppose?"

Mansus nodded.

"She went alone?"

"She took her maid, but otherwise she was alone. I thought she looked ill."

"She has been looking ill for months past," said TX, without any visible expression of sympathy. "Did she take Belinda Mary?"

Mansus was puzzled. "Belinda Mary?" he repeated slowly. "Oh, you mean the daughter? No, she's at school somewhere in France."

TX whistled a snatch of a popular song, closed the little red book with a snap and replaced it in his desk.

"I wonder where on earth people dig up names like Belinda Mary?" he mused. "Belinda Mary must be rather a weird little animal – the Lord forgive me for speaking so about my betters! If heredity counts for anything, she ought to be something between a head waiter and a pack of cards. Have you lost anything?"

Mansus was searching his pockets.

"I made a few notes, some questions I wanted to ask you about, and Lady Bartholomew was the subject of one of them. I have had her under observation for six months. Do you want it kept up?"

TX thought awhile, then shook his head.

"I am only interested in Lady Bartholomew in so far as Kara is interested in her. There is a criminal for you, my friend!" he added admiringly.

Mansus, busily engaged in going through the bundles of letters, slips of paper, and little notebooks he had taken from his pocket, sniffed audibly.

"Have you a cold?" asked TX politely.

"No, sir," was the reply, "only I haven't much opinion of Kara as a criminal. Besides, what has he got to be a criminal about? He has all that he requires in the money department, he's one of the most popular people in London, and certainly one of the best looking men I've ever seen in my life. He needs nothing."

TX regarded him scornfully.

"You're a poor blind brute," he said, shaking his head. "Don't you know that great criminals are never influenced by material desires or by the prospect of concrete gains? The man who robs his employer's till in order to give the girl of his heart the 25s pearl and ruby brooch her soul desires gains nothing but the glow of satisfaction which comes to the man who is thought well of. The majority of crimes in the world are committed by people for the same reason – they want to be thought well of. Here is Dr X, who murdered his wife because she was a drunkard and a slut, and he dare not leave her for fear the neighbours have doubts as to his respectability. Here is another gentleman who murders his wives in their baths in order that he should keep up some sort of position and earn the respect of his friends and his associates. Nothing roused him more to a frenzy of passion than the suggestion that he was not respectable. Here is the great financier who has embezzled a million and a quarter, not because he needed money but because people looked up to him. Therefore he must build great mansions, submarine pleasure courts, and must lay out huge estates – because he wished that he should be thought well of."

Mansus sniffed again.

"What about the man who half murders his wife? Does he do that to be thought well of?" he asked with a tinge of sarcasm.

TX looked at him pityingly.

"The low-brow who beats his wife, my poor Mansus," he said, "does so because she *doesn't* think well of him. That is our ruling passion, our national characteristic, the primary cause of most crimes, big or little. That is why Kara is a bad criminal, and will, as I say, end his life very violently."

He took down his glossy silk hat from the peg and slipped into his overcoat.

"I am going down to see my friend Kara," he said. "I have a feeling that I should like to talk with him. He might tell me something."

His acquaintance with Kara's *ménage* had been merely hearsay. He had interviewed the Greek once since his return, but since all his efforts to secure information concerning the whereabouts of John Lexman and his wife – the main reason for his visit – had been in vain, he had not repeated his visit.

The house in Cadogan Square was a large one, occupying a corner site. It was peculiarly English in appearance, with its window boxes, its discreet curtains, its polished brass and enamelled doorway. It had been the town house of Lord Henry Gratham, that eccentric connoisseur of wine and follower of witless pleasure. It had been built by him "round a bottle of port," as his friends said, meaning thereby that his first consideration had been the cellarage of the house, and that when those cellars had been built and provision made for the safe storage of his priceless wines, the house had been built without the architect being greatly troubled by his lordship. The double cellars of Gratham House had in their time been one of the sights of London. When Henry Gratham lay under eight feet of Congo earth (he was killed by an elephant whilst on a hunting trip), his executors had been singularly fortunate in finding an immediate purchaser. Rumour had it that Kara, who was no lover of wine, had bricked up the cellars, and their very existence passed into domestic legendary.

The door was opened by a well-dressed and deferential man-servant, and TX was ushered into the hall. A fire burnt cheerily in a bronze grate, and TX had a glimpse of a big oil-painting of Kara above the marble mantelpiece.

"Mr Kara is very busy, sir," said the man.

"Just take in my card," said TX. "I think he may care to see me."

The man bowed, produced from some mysterious corner a silver salver, and glided upstairs in that manner which well-trained servants have, a manner which seems to call for no bodily effort. In a minute he returned.

"Will you come this way, sir?" he said, and led the way up a broad flight of stairs.

At the head of the stairs was a corridor which ran to the left and to the right. From this there gave four rooms. One at the extreme end of the passage on the right, one on the left, and two at fairly regular intervals in the centre.

When the man's hand was on one of the doors TX said quietly, "I think I have seen you before somewhere, my friend."

The man smiled.

"It is very possible, sir. I was a waiter at the Constitutional for some time."

TX nodded.

"That is where it must have been," he said.

The man opened the door and announced the visitor.

TX found himself in a large room very handsomely furnished, but just lacking that sense of cosiness and comfort which is the feature of the Englishman's home.

Kara rose from behind a big writing-table, and came with a smile and a quick step to greet the visitor.

"This is a most unexpected pleasure," he said, and shook hands warmly.

TX had not seen him for a year, and found very little change in this strange young man. He could not be more confident than he had been or bear himself with a more graceful carriage. Whatever social success he had achieved it had not spoiled him, for his manner was as genial and easy as ever.

"I think that will do, Miss Holland," he said, turning to the girl who, with notebook in hand, stood by the desk.

"Evidently," thought TX, "our Hellenic friend has a pretty taste in secretaries."

In that one glance he took her all in – from the bronze-brown of her hair to her neat foot.

TX was not readily attracted by members of the opposite sex. He was self-confessed a predestined bachelor, finding life and its incidence too absorbing to give his whole mind to the serious problem of marriage, or to contract responsibilities and interests which might divert his attention from what he believed was the greater game. Yet he must be a man of stone to resist the freshness, the beauty, and the youth of this straight, slender girl; the pink and whiteness of her, the aliveness and buoyancy and the thrilling sense of vitality she carried in her very presence.

"What is the weirdest name you have ever heard?" asked Kara laughingly. "I ask you because Miss Holland and I have been discussing a begging letter addressed to us by a Maggie Goomer."

The girl smiled slightly, and in that smile was paradise, thought T X.

"The weirdest name?" he repeated. "Why, I think the worst I have heard for a long time is Belinda Mary."

"That has a familiar ring," said Kara.

TX was looking at the girl.

She was staring at him with a certain languid insolence which made him curl up inside. Then, with a glance at her employer, she swept from the room.

"I ought to have introduced you," said Kara. "That was my secretary, Miss Holland. Rather a pretty girl, isn't she?"

"Very," said TX, recovering his breath.

"I like pretty things around me," said Kara, and somehow the complacency of the remark annoyed the detective more than anything that Kara had ever said to him.

The Greek went to the mantelpiece, and taking down a silver cigarette box, opened and offered it to his visitor. Kara was wearing a grey lounge suit, and although grey is a very trying colour for a foreigner to wear, this suit fitted his splendid figure and gave him just that bulk which he needed.

"You are a most suspicious man, Mr Meredith," he smiled.

"Suspicious? I?" asked the innocent TX.

Kara nodded.

"I am sure you want to inquire into the character of all my present staff. I am perfectly satisfied that you will never be at rest until you learn the antecedents of my cook, my valet, my secretary – "

TX held up his hand with a laugh.

"Spare me," he said. "It is one of my failings, I admit, but I have never gone much farther into your domestic affairs than to pry into the antecedents of your very interesting chauffeur."

A little cloud passed over Kara's face, but it was only momentary.

"Oh, Brown," he said airily, with just a perceptible pause between the two words.

"It used to be Smith," said TX; "but no matter. His name is really Poropulos."

"Oh, Poropulos," said Kara gravely, "I dismissed him a long time ago."

"Pensioned him, too, I understand," said TX.

The other looked at him awhile; then, "I am very good to my old servants," he said slowly, and changing the subject, "To what good fortune do I owe this visit?"

TX selected a cigarette before he replied.

"I thought you might be of some service to me," he said, apparently giving his whole attention to the cigarette.

"Nothing would give me greater pleasure," said Kara a little eagerly. "I am afraid you have not been very keen on continuing what I hoped would have ripened into a valuable friendship, more valuable to me, perhaps" – he smiled – "than to you."

"I am a very shy man," said the shameless TX, "diffident to a fault, and rather apt to underrate my social attractions. I have come to you now because you know everybody. By the way, how long have you had your secretary?" he asked abruptly.

Kara looked up at the ceiling for inspiration.

"Four – no, three months," he corrected. "A very efficient young lady, who came to me from one of the training establishments. Somewhat uncommunicative, better educated than most girls in her position – for example, she speaks and writes modern Greek fairly well."

"A treasure?" suggested TX.

"Unusually so," said Kara. "She lives in Marylebone Road – 86A is the address. She has no friends, spends most of her evenings in her room, is eminently respectable and a little chilling in her attitude to her employer."

TX shot a swift glance at the other.

"Why do you tell me all this?" he asked.

"To save you the trouble of finding out," replied the other coolly. "That insatiable curiosity which is one of the equipments of your profession would, I feel sure, induce you to conduct investigations for your own satisfaction."

TX laughed.

"May I sit down?" he said.

The other wheeled an armchair across the room and TX sank into it. He leant back and crossed his legs, and was in a second the personification of ease.

"I think you are a very clever man, Monsieur Kara," he said.

The other looked down at him, this time without amusement.

"Not so clever that I can discover the object of your visit," he said pleasantly enough.

"It is very simply explained," said TX. "You know everybody in town. You know, amongst other people, Lady Bartholomew."

"I know the lady very well indeed," said Kara, readily – too readily, in fact, for the rapidity with which answer had followed question suggested to TX that Kara had anticipated the reason for the call.

"Have you any idea," asked TX, speaking with deliberation, "as to why Lady Bartholomew has gone out of town at this particular moment?"

Kara laughed.

"What an extraordinary question to ask me – as though Lady Bartholomew confided her plans to one who is little more than a chance acquaintance!"

"And yet," said TX, contemplating the burning end of his cigarette, "you know her well enough to hold her promissory note."

"Promissory note?" asked the other.

His tone was one of involuntary surprise, and TX swore softly to himself, for now he saw the faintest shade of relief in Kara's face. The Commissioner realised that he had committed an error – he had been far too definite.

"When I say promissory note," he went on easily, as though he had noticed nothing, "I mean, of course, the securities which a debtor invariably gives to one from whom he or she has borrowed large sums of money."

Kara made no answer, but opening a drawer of his desk he took out a key and brought it across to where TX was sitting.

"Here is the key of my safe," he said quietly. "You are at liberty to go carefully through its contents and discover for yourself any promissory note which I hold from Lady Bartholomew. My dear fellow, you don't imagine I'm a moneylender, do you?" he said in an injured tone.

"Nothing was farther from my thoughts," said TX untruthfully.

But the other pressed the key upon him.

"I should be awfully glad if you would look for yourself," he said earnestly. "I feel that in some way you associate Lady Bartholomew's illness with some horrible act of usury on my part. Will you satisfy yourself, and in doing so satisfy me?"

Now any ordinary man and possibly any ordinary detective would have made the conventional answer. He would have protested that he had no intention of doing anything of the sort; he would have uttered, if he were a man in the position which TX occupied, the conventional statement that he had no authority to search the private papers, and that he would certainly not avail himself of the other's kindness. But TX was not an ordinary person. He took the key and balanced it lightly in the palm of his hand.

"Is this the key of the famous bedroom safe?" he said banteringly.

Kara was looking down at him with a quizzical smile. "It isn't the safe you opened in my absence on one memorable occasion,

Mr Meredith," he said. "As you probably know, I have changed that safe; but perhaps you don't feel equal to the task?"

"On the contrary," said TX calmly, and rising from the chair, "I am going to put your good faith to the test."

For answer Kara walked to the door and opened it.

"Let me show you the way," he said politely.

He passed along the corridor and entered the apartment at the end. The room was a large one and lighted by one big square window which was protected by steel bars. In the grate, which was broad and high, a huge fire was burning, and the temperature of the room was unpleasantly close despite the coldness of the day.

"That is one of the eccentricities which you, as an Englishman, will never excuse in me," said Kara.

Near the foot of the bed, let into and flush with the wall, was a big green door of the safe.

"Here you are, Mr Meredith," said Kara. "All the precious secrets of Remington Kara are yours for the asking."

"I am afraid I've had my trouble for nothing," said TX, making no attempt to use the key.

"That is an opinion which I share," said Kara with a smile.

"Curiously enough," said TX, "I mean just what you mean."

He handed the key to Kara.

"Won't you open it?" asked the Greek.

TX shook his head.

"The safe as far as I can see is a Magnus; the key which you have been kind enough to give me has legibly inscribed upon the handle 'Chubb.' My experience as a police officer has taught me that Chubb keys very rarely open Magnus safes."

Kara uttered an exclamation of annoyance.

"How stupid of me!" he said; "yet now I remember, I sent the key to my bankers before I went out of town — I only came back this morning, you know. I will send for it at once."

"Pray don't trouble," murmured TX politely. He took from his pocket a little flat leather case and opened it. It contained a number of steel implements of curious shape which were held in position by a leather loop along the centre of the case. From one of these loops he extracted a handle, and deftly fitted something that looked like a steel awl to the socket of the handle. Looking in wonder and no little apprehension Kara saw that the awl was bent at the head.

"What are you going to do?" he asked, a little alarmed.

"I'll show you," said TX pleasantly.

Very gingerly he inserted the instrument in the small keyhole, turned it cautiously first one way and then the other. There was a sharp click followed by another. He turned the handle and the door of the safe swung open.

"Simple, isn't it?" he asked politely.

In that second of time Kara's face had undergone a transformation. The eyes which met TX Meredith's blazed with an almost insane fury. With a quick stride Kara placed himself before the open safe.

"I think this has gone far enough, Mr Meredith," he said harshly. "If you wish to search my safe you must get a warrant."

TX shrugged his shoulders, and carefully unscrewing the instrument he had employed and replacing it in the case he returned it to his inside pocket.

"It was at your invitation, my dear Monsieur Kara," he said suavely. "Of course, I knew that you were putting a bluff upon me with the key, and that you had no more intention of letting me see the inside of your safe than you had of telling me exactly what happened to John Lexman."

The shot went home.

The face which was thrust into the Commissioner's was ridged and veined with passion. The lips were turned back to show the big white even teeth, the eyes were narrowed to slits, the jaw thrust out, and almost every semblance of humanity had vanished from his face.

"You – you – " he hissed, and his clawing hands moved suspiciously backward.

"Put up your hands," said TX sharply, "and be damned quick about it!"

In a flash the hands went up, for the revolver which TX held was pressed uncomfortably against the third button of the Greek's waistcoat.

"That's not the first time you've been asked to put up your hands, I think," said TX pleasantly.

His own left hand slipped round to Kara's hip pocket. He found something in the shape of a cylinder and drew it out from the pocket. To his surprise it was not a revolver, not even a knife; it looked like a small electric torch, though instead of a bulb and a bull's-eye glass, there was a pepper-box perforation at one end.

He handled it carefully, and was about to press the small nickel knob when a strangled cry of horror broke from Kara.

"For God's sake be careful!" he gasped; "you're pointing it at me. Do not press that lever, I beg!"

"Will it explode?" asked TX curiously.

"No, no!"

TX pointed the thing downward to the carpet and pressed the knob cautiously. As he did so there was a sharp hiss, and the floor was stained with the liquid which the instrument contained. Just one gush of fluid and, no more. TX looked down. The bright carpet had already changed colour and was smoking. The room was filled with a pungent and disagreeable scent. TX looked from the floor to the white-faced man.

"Vitriol, I believe," he said, shaking his head admiringly. "What a dear little fellow you are!"

The man, big as he was, was on the point of collapse and mumbled something about self-defence, and listened without a word whilst TX, labouring under an emotion which was perfectly pardonable, described Kara, his ancestors, and the possibilities of his future estate.

Very slowly the Greek recovered his self-possession.

"I didn't intend using it on you – I swear I didn't," he pleaded. "I'm surrounded by enemies, Meredith. I had to carry some means of protection. It is because my enemies know I carry this that they fight shy of me. I'll swear I had no intention of using it on you. The idea is too preposterous. I am sorry I fooled you about the safe."

"Don't let that worry you," said TX. "I am afraid I did all the fooling. No, I cannot let you have this back again," he said as the Greek put out his hand to take the infernal little instrument. "I must take this back to Scotland Yard. It's quite a long time since we had anything new in this shape. Compressed air, I presume?"

Kara nodded solemnly.

"Very ingenious indeed," said TX. "If I had a brain like yours" – he paused – "I should do something with it – with a gun," he added as he passed out of the room.

9

My Dear Mr Meredith,

I cannot tell you how unhappy and humiliated I feel that my little joke with you should have had such an uncomfortable ending. As you know, and as I have given you proof, I have the greatest admiration in the world for one whose work for humanity has won such universal recognition.

I hope that we shall both forget this unhappy morning and that you will give me an opportunity of rendering to you in person the apologies which are due to you. I feel that anything less will neither rehabilitate me in your esteem nor secure for me the remnants of my shattered self-respect.

I am hoping you will dine with me next week and meet a most interesting man, George Gathercole, who has just returned from Patagonia – I only received his letter this morning – having made most remarkable discoveries concerning that country.

I feel sure that you are large enough minded and too much a man of the world to allow my foolish fit of temper to disturb a relationship which I have always hoped would be mutually pleasant. If you will allow Gathercole, who will be unconscious of the part he is playing, to act as peacemaker between yourself and myself, I shall feel that his trip, which has cost me a large sum of money, will not have been wasted.

I am, dear Mr Meredith,

Yours very sincerely,
Remington Kara.

Kara folded the letter and inserted it in its envelope. He rang a bell on his table, and the girl who had so filled TX with a sense of awe came from an adjoining room.

"You will see that this is delivered, Miss Holland."

She inclined her head and stood waiting. Kara rose up from his desk and began to pace the room.

"Do you know TX Meredith?" he asked suddenly.

"I have heard of him," said the girl.

"A man with a singular mind," said Kara, "a man against whom my favourite weapon would fail."

She looked at him with interest in her eyes.

"What is your favourite weapon, Mr Kara?" she asked.

"Fear," he said.

If he expected her to give him any encouragement to proceed he was disappointed. Probably he required no such encouragement, for in the presence of his social inferiors he was somewhat monopolising.

"Cut a man's flesh and it heals," he said. "Whip a man and the memory of it passes. Frighten him, fill him with a sense of foreboding and apprehension and let him believe that something dreadful is going to happen either to himself or to someone he loves – better the latter – and you will hurt him beyond forgetfulness. Fear is a tyrant and a despot, more terrible than the rack, more potent than the stake. Fear is many-eyed and sees horrors where normal vision only sees the ridiculous."

"Is that your creed?" she asked quietly.

"Part of it, Miss Holland," he smiled.

She played idly with the letter she held in her hand, balancing it on the edge of the desk, her eyes downcast.

"What would justify the use of such an awful weapon?" she asked.

"It is amply justified to secure an end," he said blandly. "For example: I want something. I cannot obtain that something through the ordinary channel or by the employment of ordinary means. It is essential to me, to my happiness, to my comfort, or my *amour propre*, that that something shall be possessed by me. If I can buy it, well and good. If I can buy those who can use their influence to secure this thing for me, so much the better. If I can obtain it by any merit I possess, I utilise that merit, providing always that I can secure my object in the time. Otherwise – "

He shrugged his shoulders.

"I see," she said, nodding her head quickly. "I suppose that is how blackmailers feel."

He frowned.

"That is a word I never use, nor do I like to hear it employed," he said. "Blackmail suggests to me a vulgar attempt to obtain money."

"Which is generally very badly wanted by the people who use it," said the girl with a little smile. "And according to your argument they are also justified."

"It is a matter of plane," he said airily. "Viewed from my standpoint, they are sordid criminals – the sort of person that TX meets, I presume, in the course of his daily work. TX," he went on somewhat oracularly, "is a man for whom I have a great deal of respect. You will probably meet him again, for he will find an opportunity of asking you a few questions about myself. I need hardly tell you – "

He lifted his shoulders with a deprecating smile.

"I shall certainly not discuss your business with any person," said the girl coldly.

"I am paying you three pounds a week, I think," he said. "I intend increasing that to five pounds because you suit me most admirably."

"Thank you," said the girl quietly, "but I am already paid quite sufficient."

She left him a little astonished and not a little ruffled.

To refuse the favours of Remington Kara was by him regarded as something of an affront. Half his quarrel with TX was that gentleman's curious indifference to the benevolent attitude which Kara had persistently adopted in his dealings with the detective.

He rang the bell, this time for his valet.

"Fisher," he said, "I am expecting a visit from a gentleman named Gathercole – a one-armed gentleman – whom you must look after if he comes. Detain him on some pretext or other, because he is rather difficult to get hold of and I want to see him. I am going out now and I shall be back at 6.30. Do whatever you can to prevent him going away until I return. He will probably be interested if you take him into the library."

"Very good, sir," said the urbane Fisher. "Will you change before you go out?"

Kara shook his head.

"I think I will go as I am," he said. "Get me my fur coat; this beastly cold kills me." He shivered as he glanced into the bleak street. "Keep my fire going, put all my private letters in my bedroom, and see that Miss Holland has her lunch."

Fisher followed him to his car, wrapped the fur rug about his legs, closed the door carefully and returned to the house. From thence onward his behaviour was somewhat extraordinary for a well-bred servant. That he should return to Kara's study and set the papers in order was natural and proper.

That he should conduct a rapid examination of all the drawers in Kara's desk might be excused on the score of diligence, since he was to some extent in the confidence of his employer.

Kara was given to making friends of his servants – up to a point. In his more generous moments, he would address his bodyguard as "Fred," and on more occasions than one, and for no apparent reason, had tipped his servant over and above his salary.

Mr Fred Fisher found little to reward him for his search until he came upon Kara's cheque book, which told him that on the previous day the Greek had drawn £6000 in cash from the bank. This interested him mightily, and he replaced the cheque book with the tightened lips and the fixed gaze of a man who was thinking rapidly. He paid a visit to the library, where the secretary was engaged in making copies of Kara's correspondence and answering letters appealing for charitable donations, and in the hack work which falls to the secretaries of the great.

He replenished the fire, asked deferentially for any instructions, and returned again to his quest. This time he made the bedroom the scene of his investigations. The safe he did not attempt to touch, but there was a small bureau in which Kara would have placed his private correspondence of the morning. This, however, yielded no result.

By the side of the bed on a small table was a telephone, the sight of which apparently afforded the servant a little amusement. This was the private phone which Kara had been instrumental in having fixed to Scotland Yard – as he had explained to his servants.

"Rum cove," said Fisher.

He paused for a moment before the closed door of the room and smilingly surveyed the great steel latch which spanned the door and fitted in an iron socket securely screwed to the framework. He lifted it gingerly – there was a little knob for the purpose – and let it fall gently into the socket which had been made to receive it on the door itself.

"Rum cove," he said again, and lifting the latch to the hook which held it up he left the room, closing the door softly behind him. He walked down the corridor with a meditative frown and began to descend the stairs to the hall.

He was less than halfway down when the one maid of Kara's household came up to meet him.

"There's a gentleman who wants to see Mr Kara," she said. "Here is his card."

Fisher took the card from the salver and read, "Mr George Gathercole, Junior Travellers' Club."

"I'll see this gentleman," he said, with a sudden brisk interest.

He found the visitor standing in the hall.

He was a man who would have attracted attention if only from the somewhat eccentric nature of his dress and his unkempt appearance. He was dressed in a well-worn overcoat of a somewhat pronounced check, he had a top hat, glossy and obviously new, at the back of his head, and the lower part of his face was covered by a ragged beard. This he was plucking with nervous jerks, talking to himself the while, and casting a disparaging eye upon the portrait of Remington Kara which hung above the marble fireplace. A pair of pince-nez sat crookedly on his nose and two fat volumes under his arm completed the picture. Fisher, who was an observer of some discernment, noticed under the overcoat a creased blue suit, large black boots, and a pair of pearl studs.

The newcomer glared round at the valet.

"Take these!" he ordered peremptorily, pointing to the books under his arm.

Fisher hastened to obey, and noted with some wonder that the visitor did not attempt to assist him either by loosening his hold of the volumes or raising his hand. Accidentally the valet's hand pressed against the other sleeve and he received a shock, for the forearm was clearly an artificial one. It was against a wooden surface beneath the sleeve that his knuckles struck, and this view of the stranger's infirmity was confirmed when the other reached round with his right hand, took hold of the gloved left hand and thrust it into the pocket of his overcoat.

"Where is Kara?" growled the stranger.

"He will be back very shortly, sir," said the urbane Fisher.

"Out, is he," boomed the visitor. "Then I shan't wait. What the devil does he mean by being out? He's had three years to be out!"

"Mr Kara expects you, sir. He told me he would be in at six o'clock at the latest."

"Six o'clock, ye gods," stormed the man impatiently. "What dog am I that I should wait till six?"

He gave a savage little tug at his beard.

"Six o'clock, eh? You will tell Mr Kara that I called. Give me those books!"

"But I assure you, sir," stammered Fisher.

"Give me those books," roared the other.

Deftly he lifted his left hand from the pocket, crooked the elbow by some quick manipulation, and thrust the books which the valet most reluctantly handed to him back to the place whence he had taken them.

"Tell Mr Kara I will call at my own time – do you understand? – at my own time. Good morning to you."

"If you would only wait, sir," pleaded the agonised Fisher.

"Wait be hanged," snarled the other. "I've waited three years, I tell you. Tell Mr Kara to expect me when he sees me!"

He went out and most unnecessarily banged the door behind him. Fisher went back to the library. The girl was sealing up some letters as he entered and looked up.

"I am afraid, Miss Holland, I've got myself into very serious trouble."

"What is that, Fisher?" asked the girl.

"There was a gentleman coming to see Mr Kara whom Mr Kara particularly wanted to see."

"Mr Gathercole," said the girl quickly.

Fisher nodded.

"Yes, miss. I couldn't get him to stay, though."

She pursed her lips thoughtfully.

"Mr Kara will be very cross, but I don't see how you could help it. I wish you had called me."

"He never gave me a chance, miss," said Fisher with a little smile. "But if he comes again I'll show him straight up to you."

She nodded.

"Is there anything you want, miss?" he asked as he stood at the door.

"What time did Mr Kara say he would be back?"

"At six o'clock, miss," the man replied.

"There is rather an important letter here which has to be delivered."

"Shall I ring up for a messenger?"

"No, I don't think that would be advisable. You had better take it yourself."

Kara was in the habit of employing Fisher as a confidential messenger when the occasion demanded such employment.

"I will go with pleasure, miss," he said.

It was a heaven-sent opportunity for Fisher, who had been inventing some excuse for leaving the house. She handed him the letter and he read without a droop of eyelid the superscription: "TX Meredith, Esq., Special Service Dept, Scotland Yard, Whitehall."

He put it carefully in his pocket and went from the room to change. Large as the house was Kara did not employ a regular staff of servants. A maid and a valet comprised the whole of the indoor staff. His cook and the other domestics necessary for conducting an establishment of that size were engaged by the day.

Kara had returned from the country earlier than had been anticipated, and save for Fisher the only other person in the house beside the girl was the middle-aged domestic who was parlour-maid, serving-maid, and housekeeper in one.

Miss Holland sat at her desk, to all appearance reading over the letters she had typed that afternoon, but her mind was very far from the correspondence before her. She heard the soft thud of the front door closing, and rising she crossed the room rapidly and looked down through the window to the street. She watched Fisher until he was out of sight, then she descended to the hall and to the kitchen.

It was not the first visit she had made to the big underground room with its vaulted roof and its great ranges – which were seldom used nowadays, for Kara gave no dinners.

The maid – who was also cook – rose up as the girl entered.

"It's a sight for sore eyes to see you in my kitchen, miss," she smiled.

"I'm afraid you're rather lonely, Mrs Beale," said the girl sympathetically.

"Lonely, miss!" cried the maid; "I fairly get the creeps sitting here hour after hour. It's that door that gives me the hump!"

She pointed to the far end of the kitchen to a solid-looking door of unpainted wood.

"That's Mr Kara's wine-cellar – nobody's been in it but him. I know he goes in sometimes, because I tried a dodge that my brother – who's a policeman – taught me. I stretched a bit of white cotton across it an' it was broke the next morning."

"Mr Kara keeps some of his private papers in there," said the girl quietly. "He has told me so himself."

"H'm," said the woman doubtfully, "I wish he'd brick it up – the same as he has the lower cellar. I get the horrors sittin' here at night

expectin' the door to open an' the ghost of the mad lord to come out
– him that was killed in Africa."

Miss Holland laughed.

"I want you to go out now," she said. "I have no stamps."

Mrs Beale obeyed with alacrity, and whilst she was assuming a hat
– being desirous of maintaining her prestige as housekeeper in the
eyes of Cadogan Square – the girl ascended to the upper floor.

Again she watched from the window the disappearing figure.

Once out of sight Miss Holland went to work with a remarkable
deliberation and thoroughness. From her bag she produced a small
purse and opened it. In the case was a new steel key. She passed swiftly
down the corridor to Kara's room and made straight for the safe.

In two seconds it was open and she was examining its contents. It
was a large safe of the usual type. There were four steel drawers fitted
at the back and at the bottom of the strong box. Two of these were
unlocked and contained nothing more interesting than accounts
relating to Kara's estate in Albania.

The top pair were locked. She was prepared for this contingency
and a second key was as efficacious as the first. An examination of the
first drawer did not produce all that she had expected. She returned
the papers to the drawer, pushed it to and locked it. She gave her
attention to the second drawer. Her hand shook a little as she pulled
it open. It was her last chance, her last hope.

There were a number of small jewel boxes almost filling the drawer.
She took them out one by one, and at the bottom she found what she
had been searching for and that which had filled her thoughts for the
past three months.

It was a square case covered in red morocco leather. She inserted
her shaking hand and took it out with a triumphant little cry.

"At last," she said aloud, and then a hand grasped her wrist, and in
a panic she turned to meet the smiling face of Kara.

10

She felt her knees shake under her and thought she was going to swoon. She put out her disengaged hand to steady herself, and if the face which was turned to him was pale, there was a steadfast resolution in her dark eyes.

"Let me relieve you of that, Miss Holland," said Kara in his silkiest tones.

He wrenched rather than took the box from her hand, replaced it carefully in the drawer, pushed the drawer to and locked it, examining the key as he withdrew it. Then he closed the safe and locked that.

"Obviously," he said presently, "I must get a new safe."

He had not released his hold of her wrist, nor did he until he had led her from the room back to the library. Then he released the girl, standing between her and the door with folded arms and that cynical, quiet, contemptuous smile of his upon his handsome face.

"There are many courses which I can adopt," he said slowly. "I can send for the police – when my servants whom you have despatched so thoughtfully have returned – or I can take your punishment into my own hands."

"So far as I am concerned," said the girl coolly, "you may send for the police."

She leant back against the edge of the desk and faced him without so much as a quaver.

"I do not like the police," mused Kara, when there came a knock at the door.

Kara turned and opened it, and after a low, strained conversation he returned, closing the door, and laid a paper of stamps on the girl's table.

"As I was saying, I do not care for the police, and I prefer my own method. In this particular instance the police obviously would not serve me, because you are not afraid of them, and in all probability you are in their pay. Am I right in supposing that you are one of TX Meredith's accomplices?"

"I do not know Mr TX Meredith," she replied calmly, "and I am not in any way associated with the police."

"Nevertheless," he persisted, "you do not seem to be very scared of them, and that removes any temptation I might have to place you in the hands of the law. Let me see – " He pursed his lips as he applied his mind to the problem.

She half sat, half stood watching him without any evidence of apprehension, but with a heart which began to quake a little. For three months she had played her part, and the strain had been greater than she had confessed to herself. Now the great moment had come and she had failed. That was the sickening, maddening thing about it all. It was not the fear of arrest or of conviction which brought a sinking to her heart; it was the despair of failure, added to a sense of her helplessness against this man.

"If I had you arrested your name would appear in all the papers, of course," he said narrowly, "and your photograph would probably adorn the Sunday journals," he added expectantly.

She laughed.

"That doesn't appal me," she said.

"I am afraid it doesn't," he replied, and strolled towards her as though to pass her on his way to the window. He was abreast of her when he suddenly swung round and, catching her in his arms, he caught her close to him. Before she could realise what he planned he had stooped swiftly and kissed her full upon the mouth.

"If you scream, I shall kiss you again," he said, "for I have sent the maid to buy some more stamps – to the General Post Office."

"Let me go," she gasped.

Now for the first time he saw the terror in her eyes, and there surged within him that mad sense of triumph, that intoxication of power which had been associated with the red letter days of his warped life.

"You're afraid!" he bantered her, half whispering the words. "You're afraid now, aren't you? If you scream I will kiss you again, do you hear?"

"For God's sake let me go," she whispered.

He felt her shaking in his arms and suddenly he released her with a little laugh, and she sank trembling from head to foot upon the chair by her desk.

"Now you're going to tell me who sent you here," he went on harshly, "and why you came. I never suspected you. I thought you were one of those strange creatures one meets in England, a gentlewoman who prefers working for her living to the more simple business of getting married. And all the time you were spying – clever – very clever!"

The girl was thinking rapidly. In five minutes Fisher would return. Somehow she had faith in Fisher's ability and willingness to save her from a situation which she realised was fraught with the greatest danger to herself. She was horribly afraid. She knew this man far better than he suspected, realised the treachery and the unscrupulousness of him. She knew he would stop short of nothing, that he was without honour and without a single attribute of goodness.

He must have read her thoughts, for he came nearer and stood over her.

"You needn't shrink, my young friend," he said with a little chuckle. "You are going to do just what I want you to do, and your first act will be to accompany me downstairs. Get up."

He half lifted, half dragged her to her feet and led her from the room. They descended to the hall together and the girl spoke no word. Perhaps she hoped that she might wrench herself free and make her escape into the street, but in this she was disappointed. The grip about her arm was a grip of steel and she knew safety did not lie in that direction. She pulled back at the head of the stairs that led down to the kitchen.

"Where are you taking me?" she asked.

"I am going to put you into safe custody," he said. "On the whole, I think it is best that the police take this matter in hand, and I shall lock you into my wine-cellar and go out in search of a policeman."

The big wooden door opened revealing a second door, and this Kara unbolted. She noticed that both doors were sheeted with steel, the outer on the inside, and the inner door on the outside. She had no time to make any further observations, for Kara thrust her into the darkness. He switched on a light.

"I will not deny you that," he said, pushing her back as she made a frantic attempt to escape. He swung the outer door to as she raised her voice in a piercing scream, and clapping his hand over her mouth held her tightly for a moment.

"I have warned you," he hissed.

She saw his face distorted with rage. She saw Kara transfigured with devilish anger, saw that handsome, almost godlike countenance thrust into hers, flushed and seamed with a malignity and a hatefulness beyond understanding, and then her senses left her and she sank limp and swooning upon the floor.

When she recovered consciousness she found herself lying on a plain stretcher bed. She sat up suddenly. Kara had gone and the door was closed. The cellar was dry and clean and its walls were enamelled white. Light was supplied by two electric lamps in the ceiling. There was a table and a chair and a small washstand, and air was evidently supplied through unseen ventilators. It was indeed a prison and no less, and in her first moments of panic she found herself wondering whether Kara had used this underground dungeon of his before for a similar purpose.

At the furthermost end was another door, and this she pushed, gently at first and then vigorously, without producing the lightest impression. She still had her bag, a small affair of black moiré, which hung from her belt, and found nothing more formidable than a penknife, a small bottle of smelling salts, and a pair of scissors. The latter she had used for cutting out those paragraphs from the daily newspapers which referred to Kara's movements.

They would make a formidable weapon, and wrapping her handkerchief round the handle to get a better grip she placed them on the table within reach. She was dimly conscious all the time that she had heard something about this wine-cellar – something which if she could recollect it would be of service to her.

Then in a flash she remembered there was a lower cellar, which according to Mrs Beale was never used and was bricked up. It was approached from the outside down a circular flight of stairs. There might be a way out from that direction, and would there not be some connection between the upper cellar and the lower?

She set to work to make a closer examination of the apartment.

The floor was of concrete covered with a light rush matting. This she carefully rolled up, starting at the door. One half of the floor was uncovered without revealing the existence of any trap. She attempted to pull the table into the centre of the room the better to roll the matting, but found it fixed to the wall, and going down on her knees she discovered that it had been fixed after the matting had been laid.

Obviously there was no need for the fixture and she tapped the floor with her little knuckle. Her heart started racing. The sound her knocking gave forth was a hollow one. She sprang up, took her bag from the table, opened the little penknife and cut carefully through the thin rushes. She might have to replace the matting and it was necessary she should do her work tidily.

Soon the whole of the trap was revealed. There was an iron ring which fitted flush with the top and which she pulled. The trap yielded and swung back as though there were a counterbalance at the other end, as indeed there was. She peered down. There was a dim light below – the reflection of a light in the distance. A flight of steps led down to the lower level, and after a second's hesitation she swung her legs over the cavity and began her descent.

She was in a cellar slightly smaller than that above her. The light she had seen came from an inner apartment which would be underneath the kitchen of the house. She made her way cautiously along, stepping on tip-toe. The first of the rooms she came to was well furnished. There was a thick carpet on the floor, comfortable easy chairs, a little bookcase well filled, and a reading-lamp. This must be Kara's underground study where he kept his precious papers. A smaller room gave from this and again it was doorless. She looked in, and after her eyes had become accustomed to the darkness she saw that it was a bathroom handsomely fitted.

The room she was in was also without any light, which came from the furthermost chamber. As the girl strode softly across the well-carpeted room she trod on something hard. She stooped and felt along the floor and her fingers encountered a thin steel chain. The girl was bewildered – almost panic-stricken. She shrunk back from the entrance of the inner room, fearful of what she would see. And then from the interior came a sound that made her tingle with horror.

It was the sound of a sigh, long and trembling. She set her teeth and strode through the doorway and stood for a moment staring with open eyes and mouth at what she saw.

"My God!" she breathed, "London!…in the twentieth century…!"

11

Superintendent Mansus had a little office in Scotland Yard proper, which he complained was not so much a private bureau as a waiting-room to which repaired every official of the police service who found time hanging on his hands. On the afternoon of Miss Holland's surprising adventure, a plainclothes man of "D" Division brought to Mr Mansus' room a very scared domestic servant, voluble, tearful and agonisingly penitent. It was a mood not wholly unfamiliar to a police officer of twenty years' experience, and Mr Mansus was not impressed.

"If you will kindly shut up," he said, blending his natural politeness with his employment of the vernacular, "and if you will also answer a few questions, it will save you a lot of trouble. You were Lady Bartholomew's maid, weren't you?"

"Yes, sir," sobbed the red-eyed Mary Ann.

"And you have been detected trying to pawn a gold bracelet, the property of Lady Bartholomew?"

The maid gulped, nodded, and started breathlessly upon a recital of her wrongs.

"Yes, sir; but she practically gave it to me, sir, and I haven't had my wages for two months, sir, and she can give that foreigner thousands and thousands of pounds at a time, sir, but her poor servants she can't pay – no, she can't. And if Sir William knew, especially about my lady's cards and about the snuffbox, what would he think, I wonder? and I'm going to have my rights, for if she can pay thousands to a swell like Mr Kara, she can pay me and – "

Mansus jerked his head.

"Take her down to the cells," he said briefly, and they led her away, a wailing, woeful figure of an amateur larcenist.

In three minutes Mansus was with TX, and had reduced the girl's incoherence to something like order.

"This is important," said TX; "produce the Abigail."

"The – ?" asked the puzzled officer.

"The skivvy – slavey – hired help – get busy," said TX impatiently.

They brought her to TX in a condition bordering upon collapse.

"Get her a cup of tea," said the wise chief. "Sit down, Mary Ann, and forget all your troubles."

"Oh, sir, I've never been in this position before," she began, as she flopped into the chair they put out for her.

"Then you've had a very tiring time," said TX. "Now listen – "

"I've been respectable – "

"Forget it!" said TX wearily. "Listen! If you'll tell me the whole truth about Lady Bartholomew and the money she paid to Mr Kara – "

"Two thousand pounds – two separate thousand, and by all accounts – "

"If you will tell me the truth I'll compound a felony and let you go free."

It was a long time before he could prevail upon her to clear her speech of the ego which insisted upon intruding. There were gaps in her narrative which he bridged. In the main it was a believable story. Lady Bartholomew had lost money and had borrowed from Kara. She had given him as security the snuffbox presented to her husband's father, a doctor, by one of the Czars for services rendered, and was "all blue enamel and gold, and foreign words in diamonds." On the question of the amount Lady Bartholomew had borrowed Abigail was very vague. All that she knew was that my lady had paid back two thousand pounds and that she was still very distressed ("in a fit" was the phrase the girl used), because apparently Kara refused to restore the box.

There had evidently been terrible scenes in the Bartholomew *ménage*, hysterics and what not, the principal breakdown having occurred when Belinda Mary came home from school in France.

"Miss Bartholomew is home then. Where is she?" asked TX.

Here the girl was more vague than ever. She thought the young lady had gone back again – anyway, Miss Belinda had been very much upset. Miss Belinda had seen Dr Williams, and advised that her mother should go away for a change.

"Miss Belinda seems to be a precocious young person," said TX; "did *she* by any chance see Mr Kara?"

"Oh, no," explained the girl. "Miss Belinda was above that sort of person. Miss Belinda was a lady if ever there was one."

"And how old is this interesting young woman?" asked TX curiously.

"She is nineteen," said the girl, and the Commissioner, who had pictured Belinda in short plaid frocks and long pigtails, and had moreover visualised her as a freckled little girl with thin legs and snub nose, was abashed.

He delivered a short lecture on the sacred rights of property, paid the girl the three months' wages which were due to her – he had no doubt as to the legality of her claim – and dismissed her with instructions to go back to the house, pack her box and clear out.

After the girl had gone TX sat down to consider the position. He might see Kara, and since Kara had expressed his contrition and was probably in a more humble state of mind, he might make reparation. Then again he might not. Mansus was waiting, and TX walked back with him to his little office.

"I hardly know what to make of it," he said in despair.

"If you can give me Kara's motive, sir, I can give you a solution," said Mansus.

TX shook his head.

"That is exactly what I am unable to give you," he said.

He perched himself on Mansus's desk and lit a cigar.

"I have a good mind to go round and see him," he said after a while.

"Why not telephone to him?" asked Mansus; "there is his phone straight into his boudoir."

He pointed to a small telephone in a corner of the room.

"Oh, he persuaded the Commissioner to run the wire, did he?" said TX, interested, and walked over to the telephone.

He fingered the receiver for a little while, and was about to take it off but changed his mind.

"I think not," he said. "I'll go round and see him tomorrow. I don't hope to succeed in extracting the confidence in the case of Lady Bartholomew which he denied me over poor Lexman."

"I suppose you'll never give up hope of seeing Mr Lexman again," smiled Mansus, busily arranging a new blotting-pad.

Before TX could answer there came a knock at the door, and a uniformed policeman entered. He saluted TX.

"They've just sent an urgent letter across from your office, sir. I said I thought you were here."

He handed the missive to the Commissioner. TX took it and glanced at the typewritten address. It was marked "Urgent" and "by hand." He took up the thin steel paper-knife from the desk and slit open the envelope. The letter consisted of three or four pages of manuscript, and, unlike the envelope, it was handwritten.

"My dear TX," it began, and the handwriting was familiar.

Mansus watching the Commissioner saw the puzzled frown gather on his superior's forehead, saw the eyebrows arch and the mouth open in astonishment, saw him hastily turn to the last page to read the signature, and then – "Howling apples!" gasped TX. "It's from John Lexman!"

His hand shook as he turned the closely written pages. The letter was dated that afternoon. There was no other address than "London."

MY DEAR TX [*it began*], I do not doubt that this letter will give you a little shock, because most of my friends will have believed that I am gone beyond return. Fortunately or unfortunately that is not so. For myself I could wish – but I am not going to take a very gloomy view since I am genuinely pleased at the thought that I shall be meeting you again. Forgive this letter if it is incoherent, but I have only this moment returned and am writing at the Charing Cross Hotel. I am not staying here, but I will let you have my address later. The crossing has been a very severe one, so you must forgive me if my letter sounds a little disjointed. You will be sorry to hear that my dear wife is dead. She died abroad about six months ago. I do not wish to talk very much about it, so you will forgive me if I do not tell you any more.

My principal object in writing to you at the moment is an official one. I suppose I am still amenable to punishment, and I have decided to surrender myself to the authorities tonight. You used to have a most excellent assistant in Superintendent Mansus, and if it is convenient to you, as I hope it will be, I will report myself to him at 10.15. At any rate, my dear TX, I do not wish to mix you up in my affairs, and if you will let me do this business through Mansus I shall be very much obliged to you.

I know there is no great punishment awaiting me, because my pardon was apparently signed on the night before my escape. I shall not have much to tell you, because there is not much in the past two years that I would care to recall. We endured a great deal of unhappiness, and death was very merciful when it took my beloved from me.

Do you ever see Kara in these days?

Will you tell Mansus to expect me at between ten and half-past, and if he will give instructions to the officer on duty in the hall I will come straight up to his room.

With affectionate regards, my dear fellow,

I am,

Yours sincerely,
JOHN LEXMAN.

TX read the letter over twice, and his eyes were troubled.

"Poor girl!" he said softly, and handed the letter to Mansus.

"He evidently wants to see you because he is afraid of using my friendship to his advantage. I shall be here, nevertheless."

"What will be the formality?" asked Mansus.

"There will be no formality," said the other briskly. "I will secure the necessary pardon from the Home Secretary, and in point of fact I have already it promised, in writing."

He walked back to Whitehall, his mind fully occupied with the momentous events of the day. It was a raw February evening, sleet was falling in the street, a piercing easterly wind drove even through his thick overcoat.

He peered forward through the semi-darkness as he neared the door of his offices.

Somebody was standing in the entrance, but it was obviously a very respectable somebody – a dumpy, motherly somebody in a seal-skin coat and a preposterous bonnet.

"Hullo," said TX in surprise, "are you trying to get in here?"

"I want to see Mr Meredith," said the visitor, in the mincing, affected tones of one who excused the vulgar source of her prosperity by frequently reiterated claims to having seen better days.

"Your longing shall be gratified," said TX gravely.

He unlocked the heavy door, passed through the uncarpeted passage – there are no frills on Government offices – and led the way up the stairs to the suite on the first floor which constituted his bureau.

He switched on all the lights and surveyed his visitor, a comfortable person of the landlady type.

"A good sort," thought TX, "but somewhat overweighted with lorgnettes and seal-skin."

"You will pardon my coming to see you at this hour of the night," she began deprecatingly, "but as my dear father used to say, 'Honi soit qui mal y pense.'"

"Your dear father being in the garter business," suggested TX humorously. "Won't you sit down, Mrs – "

"Mrs Cassley," beamed the lady as she seated herself. "He was in the paper-hanging business. But needs must when the devil drives, as the saying goes."

"What particular devil is driving you, Mrs Cassley?" asked TX, somewhat at a loss to understand the object of this visit.

"I may be doing wrong," began the lady, pursing her lips, "and two blacks will never make a white."

"And all that glitters is not gold," suggested TX a little wearily. "Will you please tell me your business, Mrs Cassley? I am a very hungry man."

"Well, it's like this, sir," said Mrs Cassley, dropping her erudition, and coming down to bedrock homeliness. "I've got a young lady stopping with me, as respectable a gel as I've had to deal with. And I know what respectability is, I might tell you, for I've taken professional boarders, and I have been housekeeper to a doctor."

"You are well qualified to speak," said TX with a smile. "And what about this particular young lady of yours? By the way, what is your address?"

"85a, Marylebone Road," said the lady.

TX sat up.

"Yes?" he said quickly. "What about your young lady?"

"She works, as far as I can understand," said the loquacious landlady, "with a certain Mr Kara, in the typewriting line. She came to me four months ago."

"Never mind when she came to you," said TX impatiently; "have you a message from the lady?"

"Well, it's like this, sir," said Mrs Cassley, leaning forward confidentially and speaking in the hollow tone which she had decided should accompany any revelation to a police officer, "this young lady said to me, 'If I don't come home any night by eight o'clock you must go to TX and tell him – '"

She paused dramatically.

"Yes, yes," said TX quickly, "for heaven's sake go on, woman."

" 'Tell him,' " said Mrs Cassley, " 'that Belinda Mary – '"

He sprang to his feet.

"Belinda Mary!" he breathed, "Belinda Mary!"

In a flash he saw it all. This girl with a knowledge of modern Greek, who was working in Kara's house, was there for a purpose. Kara had something of her mother's – something that was vital, and which he would not part with, and she had adopted this method of securing that something. Mrs Cassley was prattling on, but her voice was merely a haze of sound to him. It brought a strange glow to his heart that Belinda Mary should have thought of him.

"Only as a policeman, of course," said the still small voice of his official self. "Perhaps!" said the human TX defiantly. He got on the telephone to Mansus and gave a few instructions.

"You stay here," he ordered the astounded Mrs Cassley, "I am going to make a few investigations."

Kara was at home, but was in bed. TX remembered that this extraordinary man invariably went to bed early and that it was his practice to receive visitors in this guarded room of his. He was admitted almost at once and found Kara in his silk dressing-gown lying on the bed smoking. The heat of the room was unbearable even on that bleak February night.

"This is a pleasant surprise," said Kara, sitting up. "I hope you don't mind my *déshabillé*."

TX came straight to the point.

"Where is Miss Holland?" he asked.

"Miss Holland?" Kara's eyebrows advertised his astonishment. "What an extraordinary question to ask me, my dear man! At her home, or at the theatre, or in a cinema palace – I don't know how these people employ their evenings."

"She is not at home," said TX, "and I have reason to believe that she has not left this house."

"What a suspicious person you are, Mr Meredith!"

Kara rang the bell and Fisher came in with a cup of coffee on a tray.

"Fisher," drawled Kara, "Mr Meredith is anxious to know where Miss Holland is. Will you be good enough to tell him? you know more about her movements than I do."

"As far as I know, sir," said Fisher deferentially, "she left the house about 5.30, her usual hour. She sent me out a little before five on a message, and when I came back her hat and her coat had gone, so I presume she had gone also."

"Did you see her go?" asked TX.

The man shook his head.

"No, sir, I very seldom see the lady come or go. There has been no restrictions placed upon the young lady and she has been at liberty to move about as she likes. I think I am correct in saying that, sir?" He turned to Kara.

Kara nodded.

"You will probably find her at home."

He shook his finger waggishly at TX.

"What a dog you are," he gibed. "I ought to keep the beauties of my household veiled as we do in the East, and especially when I have a susceptible policeman wandering at large."

TX gave jest for jest. There was nothing to be gained by making trouble here. After a few amiable commonplaces he took his departure. He found Mrs Cassley being entertained by Mansus with a wholly fictitious description of the famous criminals he had arrested.

"I can only suggest that you go home," said TX. "I will send a police officer with you to report to me, but in all probability you will find the lady has returned. She may have had a difficulty in getting a bus on a night like this."

A detective was summoned from Scotland Yard and, accompanied by him, Mrs Cassley returned to her domicile with a certain importance. TX looked at his watch. It was a quarter to ten.

"Whatever happens, I must see old Lexman," he said; "tell the best men we've got in the department to stand by for eventualities. This is going to be one of my busy days."

12

Kara lay back on his down pillows with a sneer on his face and his brain very busy. What started the train of thought he did not know, but at that moment his mind was very far away. It carried him back a dozen years to a dirty little peasants' cabin on the hillside outside Durazzo; to the livid face of a young Albanian chief, who had lost at Kara's whim all that life held for a man; to the hateful eyes of the girl's father who stood with folded arms glaring down at the bound and manacled figure on the floor; to the smoke-stained rafters of this peasant cottage and the dancing shadows on the roof; to that terrible hour of waiting when he sat bound to a post with a candle flickering and spluttering lower and lower to the little heap of gunpowder that would start the train toward the clumsy infernal machine under his chair.

He remembered the day well, because it was Candlemas Day, and this was the anniversary. He remembered other things more pleasant – the beat of hoofs on the rocky roadway, the crash of the door falling in when the Turkish gendarme had battered a way to his rescue. He remembered with a savage joy the spectacle of his would-be assassins twitching and struggling on the gallows at Pezaro and – he heard the faint tinkle of the front doorbell.

Had TX returned? He slipped from the bed and went to the door, opened it slightly and listened. TX with a search warrant might be a source of panic, especially if – he shrugged his shoulders. He had satisfied TX and allayed his suspicions. He would get Fisher out of the way that night and make sure.

97

The voice from the hall below was loud and gruff. Who could it be? Then he heard Fisher's foot on the stairs and the valet entered.

"Will you see Mr Gathercole now?"

"Mr Gathercole?"

Kara breathed a sigh of relief and his face was wreathed in smiles.

"Why, of course. Tell him to come up. Ask him if he minds seeing me in my room."

"I told him you were in bed, sir, and he used shocking language," said Fisher.

Kara laughed.

"Send him up," he said; and then, as Fisher was going out of the room, he called him back.

"By the way, Fisher, after Mr Gathercole has gone, you may go out for the night. You've got somewhere to go, I suppose, and you needn't come back until the morning."

"Yes, sir," said the servant.

Such an instruction was remarkably pleasing to him. There was much that he had to do, and that night's freedom would assist him materially.

"Perhaps" – Kara hesitated – "perhaps you had better wait until eleven o'clock. Bring me up some sandwiches and a large glass of milk. Or, better still, place them on a plate in the hall."

"Very good, sir," said the man, and withdrew.

Down below that grotesque figure with his shiny hat and his ragged beard was walking up and down the tesselated hallway muttering to himself and staring at the various objects in the hall with a certain amusing antagonism.

"Mr Kara will see you sir," said Fisher.

"Oh!" said the other, glaring at the unoffending Fisher, "that's very good of him! Very good of this person to see a scholar and a gentleman who has been about his dirty business for three years. Grown grey in his service! Do you understand that, my man?"

"Yes, sir," said Fisher.

"Look here!"

The man thrust out his face.

"Do you see those grey hairs in my beard?"

The embarrassed Fisher grinned.

"Is it grey?" challenged the visitor with a roar.

"Yes, sir," said the valet hastily.

"Is it real grey?" insisted the visitor; "pull one out and see!"

The startled Fisher drew back with an apologetic smile.

"I couldn't think of doing a thing like that, sir."

"Oh, you couldn't," sneered the visitor, "then lead on!"

Fisher showed the way up the stairs. This time the traveller carried no books. His left arm hung limply by his side, and Fisher privately gathered that the hand had got loose from the detaining pocket without its owner being aware of the fact. He pushed open the door and announced "Mr Gathercole," and Kara came forward with a smile to meet his agent, who, with top hat still on the top of his head, and his overcoat dangling about his heels, must have made a remarkable picture.

Fisher closed the door behind them and returned to his duties in the hall below. Ten minutes later he heard the door opened and the booming voice of the stranger came down to him. Fisher went up the stairs to meet him and found him addressing the occupant of the room in his own eccentric fashion.

"No more Patagonia," he roared, "no more Tierra del Fuego!" he paused.

"Certainly!" he replied to some question, "but not Patagonia," he paused again, and Fisher, standing at the foot of the stairs, wondered what had occurred to make the visitor so genial.

"I suppose your cheque will be honoured all right?" asked the visitor sardonically, and then burst into a little chuckle of laughter as he carefully closed the door.

He came down the corridor talking to himself and greeted Fisher.

"Damn all Greeks," he said jovially, and Fisher could do no more than smile reproachfully, the smile being his very own, the reproach being on behalf of the master who paid him.

The traveller touched the other on the chest with his right hand.

"Never trust a Greek," he said, "always get your money in advance. Is that clear to you?"

"Yes, sir," said Fisher; "but I think you will find that Mr Kara is always most generous about money."

"Don't you believe it, don't you believe it, my poor man," said the other, "you – "

At that moment there came from Kara's room a faint "clang."

"What's that?" asked the visitor, a little startled.

"Mr Kara's put down his steel latch," said Fisher with a smile, "which means that he is not to be disturbed until – " he looked at his watch, "until eleven o'clock, at any rate."

"He's a funk!" snapped the other, "a beastly funk!"

He stamped down the stairs as though testing the weight of every tread, opened the front door without assistance, slammed it behind him and disappeared into the night.

Fisher, his hands in his pockets, looked after the departing stranger, nodding his head in reprobation.

"You're a queer old devil," he said, and looked at his watch again.

It wanted five minutes to ten.

13

"If you would care to come in, sir, I'm sure Lexman would be glad to see you," said TX, "it's very kind of you to take an interest in the matter."

The Chief Commissioner of Police growled something about being paid to take an interest in everybody, and strolled with TX down one of the apparently endless corridors of Scotland Yard.

"You won't have any bother about the pardon," he said. "I was dining tonight with old man Bartholomew and he will fix that up in the morning."

"There will be no necessity to detain Lexman in custody?" asked TX.

The Chief shook his head.

"None whatever," he said.

There was a pause, then – "By the way, did Bartholomew mention Belinda Mary?"

The white-haired Chief looked round in astonishment.

"And who the devil is Belinda Mary?" he asked.

TX went red.

"Belinda Mary," he said a little quickly, "is Bartholomew's daughter."

"By Jove," said the Commissioner, "now you mention it, he did – she is still in France."

"Oh, is she?" said TX innocently, and in his heart of hearts he wished most fervently that she was. They came to the room which Mansus occupied and found that admirable man waiting.

Wherever policemen meet, their conversation naturally drifts to "shop," and in two minutes the three were discussing with some animation and much difference of opinion, as far as TX was concerned, a series of frauds which had been perpetrated in the Midlands, and which have nothing to do with the story.

"Your friend is late," said the Chief Commissioner.

"There he is," cried TX, springing up. He heard a familiar footstep on the flagged corridor and sprung out of the room to meet the newcomer.

For a moment he stood wringing the hand of this grave man, his heart too full for words.

"My dear chap!" he said at last, "you don't know how glad I am to see you."

John Lexman said nothing, then – "I am sorry to bring you into this business, TX," he said quietly.

"Nonsense," said the other, "come in and see the Chief."

He took John by the arm and led him into the Superintendent's room.

There was a change in John Lexman, a subtle shifting of balance which was not readily discoverable. His face was older, the mobile mouth a little more grimly set, the eyes more deeply lined. He was in evening dress and looked, as TX thought, a typical clean English gentleman, such a one as any self-respecting valet would be proud to say he had "turned out."

TX looking at him carefully could see no great change save that down one side of his smooth-shaven cheek ran the scar of an old wound, which could not have been much more than superficial.

"I must apologise for this kit," said John, taking off his overcoat and laying it across the back of a chair, "but the fact is I was so bored this evening that I had to do something to pass the time away, so I dressed and went to the theatre – and was more bored than ever."

TX noticed that he did not smile, and that when he spoke it was slowly and carefully, as though he were weighing the value of every word.

"Now," he went on, "I have come to deliver myself into your hands."

"I suppose you have not seen Kara?" said TX.

"I have no desire to see Kara," was the short reply.

"Well, Mr Lexman," broke in the Chief, "I don't think you are going to have any difficulty about your escape. By the way, I suppose it was by aeroplane."

Lexman nodded.

"And you had an assistant?"

Again Lexman nodded.

"Unless you press me I would rather not discuss the matter for some little time, Sir George," he said, "there is much that will happen before the full story of my escape is made known."

Sir George nodded.

"We will leave it at that," he said cheerily, "and now I hope you have come back to delight us all with one of your wonderful plots."

"For the time being I have done with wonderful plots," said John Lexman in that even, deliberate tone of his; "I hope to leave London next week for New York and take up such of the threads of life as remain. The greater thread has gone."

The Chief Commissioner understood.

The silence which followed was broken by the loud and insistent ringing of the telephone bell.

"Hullo," said Mansus, rising quickly, "that's Kara's bell."

With two quick strides he was at the telephone and lifted down the receiver.

"Hullo," he cried. "Hullo," he cried again.

There was no reply, only the continuous buzzing, and when he hung the receiver again, the bell continued ringing.

The three policemen looked at one another.

"There's trouble there," said Mansus.

"Take off the receiver," said TX, "and try again."

Mansus obeyed, but there was no response.

"I am afraid this is not my affair," said John Lexman, gathering up his coat. "What do you wish me to do, Sir George?"

"Come along tomorrow morning and see us, Lexman," said Sir George, offering his hand.

"Where are you staying?" asked TX.

"At the Great Midland," replied the other, "at least my bags have gone on there."

"I'll come along and see you tomorrow morning. It's curious this should have happened the night you returned," he said, gripping the other's shoulder affectionately.

John Lexman did not speak for the moment.

"If anything happened to Kara," he said slowly, "if the worst that was possible happened to him, believe me I should not weep."

TX looked down into the other's eyes sympathetically.

"I think he has hurt you pretty badly, old man," he said gently.

John Lexman nodded.

"He has, damn him!" he said between his teeth.

The Chief Commissioner's motor-car was waiting outside, and in this TX, Mansus and a detective-sergeant were whirled off to Cadogan Square. Fisher was in the hall when they rang the bell and opened the door instantly.

He was frankly surprised to see his visitors. Mr Kara was in his room, he explained resentfully, as though TX should have been aware of the fact without being told. He had heard no bell ringing and, indeed, had not been summoned to the room.

"I have to see him at eleven o'clock," he said, "and I have had standing instructions not to go to him unless I am sent for."

TX led the way upstairs, and went straight to Kara's room. He knocked, but there was no reply. He knocked again, and on this failing to evoke any response, kicked heavily at the door.

"Have you a telephone downstairs?" he asked.

"Yes, sir," replied Fisher.

TX turned to the detective-sergeant.

"Phone to the Yard," he said, "and get a man up with a bag of tools. We shall have to pick this lock, and I haven't got my case with me."

"Picking the lock would be no good, sir," said Fisher, an interested spectator. "Mr Kara's got the latch down."

"I forgot that," said TX. "Tell him to bring his saw; we'll have to cut through the panel here."

While they were waiting for the arrival of the police officer, TX strove to attract the attention of the inmates of the room, but without success.

"Does he take opium or anything?" asked Mansus.

Fisher shook his head.

"I've never known him to take any of that kind of stuff," he said.

TX made a rapid survey of the other rooms on that floor. The room next to Kara's was the library, beyond that was a dressing-room which, according to Fisher, Miss Holland had used, and at the farthermost end of the corridor was the dining-room.

Facing the dining-room was a small service lift, and by its side a store-room in which were a number of trunks, including a very large one smothered in injunctions in three different languages to "handle with care." There was nothing else of interest on this floor; and the upper and lower floors could wait. In a quarter of an hour the carpenter had arrived from Scotland Yard, had bored a hole in the rosewood panel of Kara's room, and was busily applying his slender saw.

Through the hole he cut TX could see no more than that the room was in darkness save for the glow of a blazing fire. He inserted his hand, groped for the knob of the steel latch, which he had remarked on his previous visit to the room, lifted it, and the door swung open.

"Keep outside, everybody," he ordered.

He felt for the switch of the electric, found it, and instantly the room was flooded with light. The bed was hidden by the open door. TX took one stride into the room and saw enough. Kara was lying half on and half off the bed. He was quite dead, and the blood-stained patch above his heart told its own story.

TX stood looking down at him, saw the frozen horror on the dead man's face, then drew his eyes away and slowly surveyed the room. There in the middle of the carpet he found his clue, a bent and twisted little candle such as you find on children's Christmas trees.

14

It was Mansus who found the second candle, a stouter affair. It lay underneath the bed. The telephone, which stood on a fairly large-sized table by the side of the bed, was overturned, and the receiver was on the floor. By its side were two books, one being *The Balkan Question*, by Villari, and the other *Travels and Politics in the Near East*, by Miller. With them was a long ivory paper-knife.

There was nothing else on the bedside table save a silver cigarette-box. TX drew on a pair of gloves and examined the bright surface for finger-prints; but a superficial view revealed no such clue.

"Open the window," said TX, "the heat here is intolerable. Be very careful, Mansus. By the way, is the window fastened?"

"Very well fastened," said the superintendent, after a careful scrutiny.

He pushed back the fastenings, lifted the window, and as he did so a harsh bell rang in the basement.

"That is the burglar alarm, I suppose," said TX. "Go down and stop that bell."

He addressed Fisher, who stood with a troubled face at the door. When he had disappeared TX gave a significant glance to one of the waiting officers, and the man sauntered after the valet.

Fisher stopped the bell and came back to the hall and stood before the hall fire, a very troubled man. Near the fire was a big oaken writing-table, and on this there lay a small envelope which he did not remember having seen before, though it might have been there for some time, for he had spent the greater portion of the evening in the kitchen with the cook.

He picked up the envelope and with a start recognised that it was addressed to himself. He opened it and took out a card. There were only a few words written upon it, but they were sufficient to banish all the colour from his face and set his hands shaking. He took the envelope and card and flung them into the fire.

It so happened that at that moment Mansus had called from upstairs, and the officer who had been told off to keep the valet under observation ran up in answer to the summons. For a moment Fisher hesitated, then, hatless and coatless as he was, he crept to the door, opened it, leaving it ajar behind him, and, darting down the steps, ran like a hare from the house.

The doctor who came a little later was cautious as to the hour of death.

"If you got your telephone message at 10.25, as you say, that was probably the hour he was killed," he said. "I could not tell within half an hour. Obviously the man who killed him gripped his throat with his left hand – there are the bruises on his neck – and stabbed him with the right."

It was at this time that the disappearance of Fisher was noticed, but the cross-examination of the terrified Mrs Beale removed any doubt that TX had as to the man's guilt.

"You had better send out an 'All Stations' message and pull him in," said TX. "He was with the cook from the moment the visitor left until a few minutes before we rang. Besides which it is obviously impossible for anybody to have got into this room or out again. Have you searched the dead man?"

Mansus produced a tray on which Kara's belongings had been disposed. The ordinary keys Mrs Beale was able to identify. There were one or two which were beyond her. TX recognised one of these as the key of the safe, but two smaller keys baffled him not a little, and Mrs Beale was at first unable to assist him.

"The only thing I can think of, sir," she said, "is the wine-cellar."

"The wine-cellar?" said TX slowly, "that must be –" He stopped.

The greater tragedy of the evening, with all its mystifying aspects, had not banished from his mind the thought of the girl – that Belinda

Mary, who had called upon him in her hour of danger, as he divined. Perhaps – he descended into the kitchen and was brought face to face with the unpainted door.

"It looks more like a prison than a wine-cellar," he said.

"That's what I've always thought, sir," said Mrs Beale, "and sometimes I've had a horrible feeling of fear."

He cut short her loquacity by inserting one of the keys in the lock – it did not turn, but he had more success with the second. The lock snapped back easily, and he pulled the door back. He found the inner door bolted top and bottom. The bolts slipped back in their well-oiled sockets without any effort. Evidently Kara used this place pretty frequently, thought TX.

He pushed the door open and stopped with an exclamation of surprise. The cellar apartment was brilliantly lit – but it was unoccupied.

"This beats the band," said TX.

He saw something on the table and lifted it up. It was a pair of long-bladed scissors, and about the handle was wound a handkerchief. It was not this fact which startled him, but that the scissors blades were dappled with blood, and blood, too, was on the handkerchief. He unwound the flimsy piece of cambric and stared at the monogram, "B M B."

He looked round. Nobody had seen the weapon; and he dropped it in his overcoat pocket, and walked from the cellar to the kitchen, where Mrs Beale and Mansus awaited him.

"There is a lower cellar, is there not?" he asked in a strained voice.

"That was bricked up when Mr Kara took the house," explained the woman.

"There is nothing more to look for here," he said.

He walked slowly up the stairs to the library, his mind in a whirl. That he, an accredited officer of police, sworn to the business of criminal detection, should attempt to screen one who was conceivably a criminal was inexplicable. But if the girl had committed this crime, how had she reached Kara's room, and why had she returned to the locked cellar?

He sent for Mrs Beale to interrogate her. She had heard nothing; and she had been in the kitchen all the evening. One fact she did reveal, however, that Fisher had gone from the kitchen and had been absent a quarter of an hour, and had returned a little agitated.

"Stay here," said TX, and went down again to the cellar to make a further search.

"Probably there is some way out of this subterranean goal," he thought; and a diligent search of the room soon revealed it.

He found the iron trap, pulled it open, and slipped down the stairs. He, too, was puzzled by the luxurious character of the vault. He passed from room to room and finally came to the inner chamber, where a light was burning.

The light, as he discovered, proceeded from a small reading-lamp which stood by the side of a small brass bedstead. The bed had recently been slept in, but there was no sign of any occupant. TX conducted a very careful search, and had no difficulty in finding the bricked-up door. Other exits there were none.

The floor was of wood block laid on concrete, the ventilation was excellent, and in one of the recesses, which had evidently held at some time or other a large wine-bin, there was a perfect electrical cooking plant. In a small larder were a number of baskets bearing the name of a well-known caterer, one of them containing an excellent assortment of cold and potted meats, preserves, etc.

TX went back to the bedroom and took the little lamp from the table by the side of the bed and began a more careful examination. Presently he found traces of blood, and followed an irregular trail to the outer room. He lost it suddenly at the foot of stairs leading down from the upper cellar. Then he struck it again. He had reached the end of his electric flex and was now depending upon an electric torch he had taken from his pocket.

There were indications of something heavy having been dragged across the room; and he saw that it led to a small bathroom. He had made a cursory examination of this well-appointed apartment, and now he proceeded to make a close investigation and was well rewarded.

The bathroom was the only apartment which possessed anything resembling a door – a twofold screen – and as he pressed this back, he felt something which prevented its wider extension. He slipped into the room and flashed his lamp in the space behind the screen. There, stiff in death, with glazed eyes and lolling tongue, lay a great gaunt dog, his yellow fangs exposed in a last grimace.

About the neck was a collar, and attached to that a few links of broken chain. TX mounted the steps thoughtfully and passed out to the kitchen.

Did Belinda Mary stab Kara or kill the dog? That she killed one hound or the other was certain. That she killed both was possible.

15

After a busy and sleepless night he came down to report to the Chief Commissioner the next morning. The evening newspaper bills were filled with the "Chelsea Sensation," but the information given was of a meagre character.

"So far," reported TX to his superior, "I have been unable to trace either Gathercole or the valet. The only thing we know about Gathercole is that he sent his article to *The Times* with his card. The servants of his Club are very vague as to his whereabouts. He is a very eccentric man who only comes in occasionally, and the steward whom I interviewed says that it frequently happened that Gathercole arrived and departed without anybody being aware of the fact. We have been to his old lodgings in Lincoln's Inn, but apparently he sold up there before he went away to the wilds of Patagonia and relinquished his tenancy. The only clue I have is that a man answering to some extent to his description left by the eleven o'clock train for Paris last night."

"You have seen the secretary, of course?" said the Chief.

It was a question which TX had been dreading.

"Gone too," he answered shortly; "in fact she has not been seen since 5.30 yesterday evening."

Sir George leant back in his chair and rumpled his thick grey hair.

"The only person who seems to have remained," he said with heavy sarcasm, "was Kara himself. Would you like me to put somebody else on this case – it isn't exactly your job – or will you carry it on?"

"I prefer to carry it on, sir," said TX firmly.

"Have you found out anything more about Kara?"

TX nodded.

"All that I have discovered about him is eminently discreditable," he said. "He seems to have had an ambition to occupy a very important position in Albania. To this end he has bribed and subsidised the Turkish and Albanian officials, and has a fairly large following in that country. Bartholomew tells me that Kara had already sounded him as to the possibility of the British Government recognising a *fait accompli* in Albania, and had been inducing him to use his influence with the Cabinet to recognise the consequence of any revolution. There is no doubt whatever that Kara has engineered all the political assassinations which have been such a feature in the news from Albania during this past year. We also found in the house very large sums of money and documents which we have handed over to the Foreign Office for decoding."

Sir George thought for a long time, then he said: "I have an idea that if you find your secretary you will be halfway to solving the mystery."

TX went out from the office in anything but a joyous mood. He was on his way to lunch when he remembered his promise to call upon John Lexman.

Could Lexman supply a key which would unravel this tragic tangle? He leant out of his taxi-cab and re-directed the driver. It happened that the cab drove up to the door of the Great Midland Hotel as John Lexman was coming out.

"Come and lunch with me," said TX. "I suppose you've heard all the news."

"I read about Kara being killed, if that's what you mean," said the other. "It was rather a coincidence that I should have been discussing the matter last night at the very moment when his telephone bell rang – I wish to heaven you hadn't been in this," he said fretfully.

"Why?" asked the astonished Assistant Commissioner, "and what do you mean by 'in it'?"

"In the concrete sense I wish you had not been present when I returned," said the other moodily. "I wanted to be finished with the whole sordid business without in any way involving my friends."

"I think you are too sensitive," laughed the other, clapping him on the shoulder. "I want you to unburden yourself to me, my dear chap, and tell me anything you can that will help me to clear up this mystery."

John Lexman looked straight ahead with a worried frown.

"I would do almost anything for you, TX," he said quietly, "the more so since I know how good you were to Grace, but I can't help you in this matter. I hated Kara living, I hate him dead," he cried, and there was a passion in his voice which was unmistakable; "he was the vilest thing that ever drew the breath of life. There was no villainy too despicable, no cruelty so horrid but that he gloried in it. If ever the devil were incarnate on earth he took the shape and the form of Remington Kara. He died too merciful a death by all accounts. But if there is a God, this man will suffer for his crime in hell through all eternity."

TX looked at him in astonishment. The hate in the man's face took his breath away. Never before had he experienced or witnessed such a vehemence of loathing.

"What did Kara do to you?" he demanded.

The other looked out of the window.

"I am sorry," he said in a milder tone, "that is my weakness. Some day I will tell you the whole story, but for the moment it were better that it were not told. I will tell you this" – he turned round and faced the detective squarely – "Kara tortured and killed my wife."

TX said no more.

Halfway through lunch he returned indirectly to the subject.

"Do you know Gathercole?" he asked.

Lexman nodded.

"I think you asked me that question once before, or perhaps it was somebody else. Yes, I know him, rather an eccentric man with an artificial arm."

"That's the cove," said TX with a little sigh, "he's one of the few men I want to meet just now."

"Why?"

"Because he was apparently the last man to see Kara alive."

John Lexman looked at the other with an impatient jerk of his shoulders.

"You don't suspect Gathercole, do you?" he asked.

"Hardly," said the other dryly; "in the first place the man that committed this murder had two hands and needed them both. No, I only want to ask that gentleman the subject of his conversation. I also want to know *who was in the room with Kara when Gathercole went in.*"

"H'm," said John Lexman.

"Even if I found who the third person was, I am still puzzled as to how they got out and fastened the heavy latch behind them. Now in the old days, Lexman," he said good-humouredly, "you would have made a fine mystery story out of this. How would you have made your man escape?"

Lexman thought for a while.

"Have you examined the safe?" he asked.

"Yes," said the other.

"Was there very much in it?"

TX looked at him in astonishment.

"Just the ordinary books and things. Why do you ask?"

"Suppose there were two doors to that safe, one on the outside of the room and one on the inside, would it be possible to pass through the safe and go down the wall?"

"I have thought of that," said TX.

"Of course," said Lexman, leaning back and toying with a salt-spoon, "in writing a story where one hasn't got to deal with the absolute possibilities, one could always have made Kara have a safe of that character in order to make his escape in the event of danger. He might keep a rope ladder stored inside, open the back door, throw out his ladder to a friend, and by some trick arrangement could detach the ladder and allow the door to swing to again."

"A very ingenious idea," said TX, "but unfortunately it doesn't work in this case. I have seen the makers of the safe, and there is nothing very eccentric about it except the fact that it is mounted as it is. Can you offer another suggestion?"

John Lexman thought again.

"I will not suggest trap doors, or secret panels, or anything so banal," he said, "nor mysterious springs in the wall which, when touched, reveal secret staircases."

He smiled slightly.

"In my early days I must confess I was rather keen upon that sort of thing, but age has brought experience, and I have discovered the impossibility of bringing an architect to one's way of thinking even in so commonplace a matter as the position of a scullery. It would be much more difficult to induce him to construct a house with double walls and secret chambers."

TX waited patiently.

"There is a possibility, of course," said Lexman slowly, "that the steel latch may have been raised by somebody outside by some ingenious magnetic arrangement and lowered in a similar manner."

"I have thought about it," said TX triumphantly, "and I have made the most elaborate tests only this morning. It is quite impossible to raise the steel latch, because once it is dropped it cannot be raised again by means of the knob, the pulling of which releases the catch which holds the bar securely in its place. Try another one, John."

John Lexman threw back his head in a noiseless laugh.

"Why I should be helping you to discover the murderer of Kara is beyond my understanding," he said; "but I will give you another theory, at the same time warning you that I may be putting you off the track. For God knows I have more reason to murder Kara than any man in the world!"

He thought a while.

"The chimney was, of course, impossible?"

"There was a big fire burning in the grate," explained TX, "so big indeed that the room was stifling."

John Lexman nodded.

"That was Kara's way," he said; "as a matter of fact I know the suggestion about magnetism in the steel bar was impossible, because I was friendly with Kara when he had that bar put in, and pretty well know the mechanism, although I have forgotten it for the moment. What is your own theory, by the way?"

TX pursed his lips.

"My theory isn't very clearly formed," be said cautiously, "but so far as it goes it is that Kara was lying on the bed, probably reading one of the books which were found by the bedside, when his assailant suddenly came upon him. Kara seized the telephone to call for assistance and was promptly killed."

Again there was silence.

"That is a theory," said John Lexman with his curious deliberation of speech, "but as I say I refuse to be definite. Have you found the weapon?"

TX shook his head.

"Were there any peculiar features about the room which astonished you, and which you have not told me?"

TX hesitated.

"There were two candles," he said, "one in the middle of the room and one under the bed. That in the middle of the room was a small Christmas candle, the one under the bed was the ordinary candle of commerce, evidently roughly cut, and probably cut in the room. We found traces of candle chips on the floor, and it is evident to me that the portion which was cut off was thrown into the fire, for here again we have a trace of grease."

Lexman nodded.

"Anything further?" he asked.

"The smaller candle was twisted into a sort of corkscrew shape."

"The Clue of the Twisted Candle," mused John Lexman. "That's a very good title. Kara hated candles."

"Why?"

Lexman leant back in his chair, and selected a cigarette from a silver case.

"In my wanderings," he said, "I have been to many strange places. I have been to the country which you probably do not know, and which the traveller who writes books about countries seldom visits. There are queer little villages perched on the spurs of the bleakest hills you ever saw. I have lived with communities which acknowledge no king and no government. These had their laws handed down to them from father to son – it is a nation without a written language. They administer their laws rigidly and drastically. The punishments they award are cruel – inhuman. I have seen the woman taken in adultery stoned to death in the best Biblical traditions, and I have seen the thief blinded."

TX shivered.

"I have seen the false witness stand up in a barbaric marketplace whilst his tongue was torn from him. Sometimes the Turks or the piebald Governments of the State sent down a few gendarmes and tried a sort of sporadic administration of the country. It usually ended in the gendarme lapsing into barbarism or else disappearing from the face of the earth, with a whole community of murderers eager to testify with singular unanimity to the fact that he had either committed suicide or had gone off with the wife of one of the townsmen.

"In some of these communities the candle plays a big part. It is not the candle of commerce as you know it, but a dip made from mutton fat. Strap three between the fingers of your hands and keep the hand rigid with two flat pieces of wood; then let the candles burn down lower and lower – can you imagine? Or set a candle in a gunpowder trail, and lead the trail to a well-oiled heap of shavings thoughtfully heaped about your naked feet. Or a candle fixed to the shaved head of a man – there are hundreds of variations, and the candle plays a part in all of them. I don't know which Kara had cause to hate the worst, but I know one or two that he has employed."

"Was he as bad as that?" asked TX.

John Lexman laughed.

"You don't know how bad he was," he said.

Towards the end of the luncheon the waiter brought a note in to TX, which had been sent on from his office.

DEAR MR MEREDITH,

In answer to your inquiry I believe my daughter is in London, but I did not know it until this morning. My banker informs me that my daughter called at the bank this morning and drew a considerable sum of money from her private account, but where she has gone and what she is doing with the money I do not know. I need hardly tell you that I am very worried about this matter, and I should be glad if you could explain what it is all about.

It was signed "William Bartholomew."

TX groaned.

"If I had only had the sense to go to the bank this morning I should have seen her," he said. "I'm going to lose my job over this."

The other looked troubled.

"You don't seriously mean that?"

"Not exactly," smiled TX, "but I don't think the Chief is very pleased with me just now. You see I have butted into this business without any authority – it isn't exactly in my department. But you have not given me your theory about the candles."

"I have no theory to offer," said the other, folding up his serviette; "the candles suggest a typical Albanian murder. I do not say that it was so, I merely say that by their presence they suggest a crime of this character."

With this TX had to be content.

If it were not his business to interest himself in commonplace murder – though this hardly fitted such a description – it was part of the peculiar function which his department exercised to restore to Lady Bartholomew a certain very elaborate snuffbox which he discovered in the safe. Letters had been found amongst his papers which made clear the part which Kara had played. Though he had not been a vulgar blackmailer he had retained his hold not only upon this particular property of Lady Bartholomew, but upon certain other articles which were discovered, with no other object, apparently, than to compel influence from quarters likely to be of assistance to him in his schemes.

The inquest on the murdered man which the Assistant Commissioner attended produced nothing in the shape of evidence, and the coroner's verdict of "murder against some person or persons unknown" was only to be expected.

TX spent a very busy and a very tiring week tracing elusive clues which led him nowhere. He had a letter from John Lexman announcing the fact that he intended leaving for the United States. He had received a very good offer from a firm of magazine publishers in New York and was going out to take up the appointment.

Meredith's plans were now in fair shape. He had decided upon the line of action he would take, and in the pursuance of this he interviewed his Chief and the Minister of Justice.

"Yes, I have heard from my daughter," said that great man uncomfortably, "and really she has placed me in a most embarrassing position. I cannot tell you, Mr Meredith, exactly in what manner she has done this, but I can assure you she has."

"Can I see her letter or telegram?" asked TX.

"I am afraid that is impossible," said the other solemnly, "she begged me to keep her communication very secret. I have written to my wife and asked her to come home. I feel the constant strain to which I am being subjected is more than human man can endure."

"I suppose," said TX patiently, "it is impossible for you to tell me to what address you have replied?"

"To no address," answered the other, and corrected himself hurriedly; "that is to say I only received the telegram – the message – this morning, and there is no address to reply to."

"I see," said TX.

That afternoon he instructed his secretary.

"I want a copy of all the agony advertisements in tomorrow's papers and in the last editions of the evening papers. Have them ready for me tomorrow morning when I come."

They were waiting for him when he reached the office at nine o'clock the next day, and he went through them carefully. Presently he found the message he was seeking.

B M – You place me awkward position. Very thoughtless. Have received package addressed your mother which have placed in mother's sitting-room. Cannot understand why you want me to go away weekend and give servants holiday, but have done so. Shall require very full explanation. Matter gone far enough. – FATHER.

"This," said TX exultantly, as he read the advertisement, "is where I get busy."

16

February, as a rule, is not a month of fogs, but rather a month of
tempestuous gales, of frosts and snowfalls, but the night of February
17th, 19—, was one of calm and mist. It was not the typical London
fog so dreaded by the foreigner, but one of those little patchy mists
which smoke through the streets, now enshrouding and making the
nearest object invisible, now clearing away to the finest diaphanous
filament of pale grey.

Sir William Bartholomew had a house in Portman Place, which is
a wide thoroughfare filled with solemn edifices of unlovely and
forbidding exterior, but remarkably comfortable within. Shortly
before eleven on the night of February 17th, a taxi drew up at the
junction of Sussex Street and Portman Place, and a girl alighted. The
fog at this moment was denser than usual, and she hesitated a moment
before she left the shelter which the cab afforded.

She gave the driver a few instructions and walked on with a firm
step, turning abruptly and mounting the steps of Number 173. Very
quickly she inserted her key in the lock, pushed the door open and
closed it behind her. She switched on the hall light. The house
sounded hollow and deserted, a fact which afforded her considerable
satisfaction. She turned the light out and found her way up the broad
stairs to the first floor, paused for a moment to switch on another light,
which she knew would not be observable from the street outside, and
mounted the second flight.

Miss Belinda Mary Bartholomew congratulated herself upon the
success of her scheme, the only doubt that was in her mind now was

whether the boudoir had been locked, but her father was rather careless in such matters, and Jacks the butler was one of those dear silly old men who never locked anything, and in consequence faced every audit with a long face and a longer tale of the peculations of occasional servants.

To her immense relief the handle turned, and the door opened to her touch. Somebody had had the sense to pull down the blinds, and the curtains were drawn. She switched on the light with a sigh of relief. Her mother's writing-table was covered with unopened letters, but she brushed these aside in her search for the little parcel. It was not there, and her heart sank. Perhaps she had put it in one of the drawers. She tried them all without result.

She stood by the desk a picture of perplexity, biting a finger thoughtfully.

"Thank goodness!" she said with a jump, for she saw the parcel on the mantelshelf, crossed the room and took it down.

With eager hands she tore off the covering and came to the familiar leather case. Not until she had opened the padded lid and had seen the snuffbox reposing in a bed of cotton wool did she relapse into a long sigh of relief.

"Thank heaven for that," she said aloud.

"And me," said a voice.

She sprung up and turned round with a look of terror.

"Mr – Mr Meredith," she stammered.

TX stood by the window curtains from whence he had made his dramatic entry upon the scene.

"I say you have to thank me also, Miss Bartholomew," he said presently.

"How do you know my name?" she asked with some curiosity.

"I know everything in the world," he answered, and she smiled. Suddenly her face went serious and she demanded sharply: "Who sent you after me – Mr Kara?"

"Mr Kara?" he repeated in wonder.

"He threatened to send for the police," she went on rapidly, "and I told him he might do so. I didn't mind the police – it was Kara I was afraid of. You know what I went for, my mother's property."

She held the snuffbox in her outstretched hand.

"He accused me of stealing and was hateful, and then he put me downstairs in that awful cellar and – "

"And?" suggested TX.

"That's all," she replied with tightened lips. "What are you going to do now?"

"I am going to ask you a few questions if I may," he said. "In the first place have you not heard anything about Mr Kara since you went away?"

She shook her head.

"I have kept out of his way," she said grimly.

"Have you seen the newspapers?" he asked.

She nodded.

"I have seen the advertisement column. I wired asking Papa to reply to my telegram."

"I know – I saw it," he smiled; "that is what brought me here."

"I was afraid it would," she said ruefully; "father is awfully loquacious in print – he makes speeches, you know. All I wanted him to say was Yes or No. What do you mean about the newspapers?" she went on. "Is anything wrong with mother?"

He shook his head.

"So far as I know Lady Bartholomew is in the best of health, and is on her way home."

"Then what do you mean by asking me about the newspapers?" she demanded. "Why should I see the newspapers – what is there for me to see?"

"About Kara?" he suggested.

She shook her head in bewilderment.

"I know and want to know nothing about Kara. Why do you say this to me?"

"Because," said TX slowly, "on the night you disappeared from Cadogan Square Remington Kara was murdered."

"Murdered!" she gasped.

He nodded.

"He was stabbed to the heart by some person or persons unknown."

TX took his hand from his pocket and pulled something out which was wrapped in tissue paper. This he carefully removed and the girl watched with fascinated gaze, and with an awful sense of apprehension. Presently the object was revealed. It was a pair of scissors with the handle wrapped about with a small handkerchief dappled with brown stains. She took a step backward, raising her hands to her cheeks.

"My scissors," she said huskily; "you won't think – "

She stared up at him, fear and indignation struggling for mastery.

"I don't think you committed the murder," he smiled, "if that's what you mean to ask me; but if anybody else found those scissors and had identified this handkerchief you would have been in rather a fix, my young friend."

She looked at the scissors and shuddered.

"I did kill – something," she said in a low voice, "an awful dog… I don't know how I did it, but the beastly thing jumped at me, and I just stabbed him and killed him, and I am glad." She nodded many times and repeated, "I am glad."

"So I gather – I found the dog, and now perhaps you'll explain why I didn't find you?"

Again she hesitated, and he felt she was hiding something from him.

"I don't know why you didn't find me," she said. "I was there."

"How did you get out?"

"How did *you* get out?" she challenged him boldly.

"I got out through the door," he confessed. "It seems a ridiculously commonplace way of leaving, but that's the only way I could see."

"And that's how I got out," she answered with a little smile.

"But it was locked."

She laughed.

"I see now," she said, "I was in the cellar. I heard your key in the lock and bolted down the trap, leaving those awful scissors behind. I thought it was Kara with some of his friends, and then the voices died away and I ventured to come up, and found you had left the door open. So I – so I – "

These queer little pauses puzzled TX. There was something she was not telling him – something she had yet to reveal.

"So I got away, you see," she went on. "I came out into the kitchen; there was nobody there, and I passed through the area door and up the steps, and just round the corner I found a taxi-cab – and that is all."

She spread out her hands in a dramatic little gesture.

"And that is all, is it?" said TX.

"That is all," she repeated. "Now what are you going to do?"

TX looked up at the ceiling and stroked his chin.

"I suppose that I ought to arrest you. I feel that something is due from me. May I ask if you were sleeping in the bed downstairs?"

"In the lower cellar?" she demanded. A little pause and then, "Yes, I was sleeping in the cellar downstairs."

There was that interval of hesitation almost between each word.

"What are you going to do?" she said again.

She was feeling more sure of herself, and had suppressed the panic which his sudden appearance had produced in her. He rumpled his hair, a gross imitation, did she but know it, of one of his chief mannerisms, and she observed that that hair was very thick and inclined to curl. She saw that he was passably good-looking, had fine grey eyes, a straight nose, and a most firm chin.

"I think," she suggested gently, "you had better arrest me."

"Don't be silly," he begged.

She stared at him in amazement.

"What did you say?" she asked wrathfully.

"I said 'Don't be silly,' " repeated the calm young man.

"Do you know that you're being very rude?" she asked.

"Am I?"

He seemed interested and surprised at this novel view of his conduct.

"Of course," she went on, carefully smoothing her dress and avoiding his eye, "I know you think I am silly, and that I've got a most comic name."

"I have never said your name was comic," he replied coldly. "I would not take so great a liberty."

"You said it was 'weird,' which was worse," she claimed.

"I may have said it was 'weird,' " he admitted, "but that's rather different from saying it was 'comic.' There is dignity in weird things. For example, nightmares aren't comic, but they're weird."

"Thank you," she said pointedly.

"Not that I mean your name is anything approaching a nightmare." He made this concession with a most magnificent sweep of hand as though he were a king conceding her the right to remain covered in his presence. "I think that Belinda Ann – "

"Belinda Mary," she corrected.

"Belinda Mary I was going to say, or, as a matter of fact," he floundered, "I was going to say Belinda and Mary."

"You were going to say nothing of the kind," she corrected him.

"Anyway, I think Belinda Mary is a very pretty name."

"You think nothing of the sort."

She saw the laughter in his eyes and felt an insane desire to laugh.

"You said it was a weird name and you think it is a weird name, but I really can't be bothered considering everybody's views. I think it's a weird name too. I was named after an aunt," she added in self-defence.

"There you have the advantage of me," he inclined his head politely, "I was named after my father's favourite dog."

"What does TX stand for?" she asked curiously.

"Thomas Xavier," he said; and she leant back in the big chair on the edge of which a few minutes before she had perched herself in trepidation and dissolved into a fit of immoderate laughter.

"It is comic, isn't it?" he asked.

"Oh, I am sorry I'm so rude," she gasped. "Fancy being called Tommy Xavier – I mean, Thomas Xavier."

"You may call me Tommy if you wish – most of my friends do."

"Unfortunately I'm not your friend," she said, still smiling and wiping the tears from her eyes, "so I shall go on calling you Mr Meredith if you don't mind."

She looked at her watch.

"If you are not going to arrest me I'm going," she said.

"I have certainly no intention of arresting you," said he, "but I am going to see you home."

She jumped up smartly. You're not," she commanded.

She was so definite in this that he was startled.

"My dear child," he protested.

"Please don't 'dear child' me," she said seriously; "you're going to be a good little Tommy and let me go home by myself."

She held out her hand frankly and the laughing appeal in her eyes was irresistible.

"Well, I'll see you to a cab," he insisted.

"And listen while I give the driver instructions where he is to take me?"

She shook her head reprovingly. "It must be an awful thing to be a policeman."

He stood back with folded arms, a stern frown on his face.

"Don't you trust me?" he asked.

"No," she replied.

"Quite right," he approved; "anyway I'll see you to the cab and you can tell the driver to go to Charing Cross station, and on your way you can change your direction."

"And you promise you won't follow me?" she asked.

"On my honour," he swore. "On one condition though."

"I will make no conditions," she replied haughtily.

"Please come down from your great big horse," he begged, "and listen to reason. The condition I make is that I can always bring you to an appointed *rendezvous* whenever I want you. Honestly this is necessary, Belinda Mary."

"Miss Bartholomew," she corrected coldly.

"It is necessary," he went on, "as you will understand. Promise me that if I put an advertisement in the agonies of either an evening paper which I will name, or in the *Morning Post*, you will keep the appointment I fix, if it is humanly possible."

She hesitated a moment, then held out her hand.

"I promise," she said.

"Good for you, Belinda Mary," said he, and tucking her arm in his he led her out of the room, switching off the light and racing her down the stairs.

"Good night," he said, holding her hand.

"That's the third time you've shaken hands with me tonight," she interjected.

"Don't let us have any unpleasantness at the last," he pleaded, "and remember."

"I have promised," she replied.

"And one day," he went on, "you will tell me all that happened in that cellar."

"I have told you," she said in a low voice.

"You have not told me everything, child."

He handed her into the cab. He shut the door behind her and leant through the open window.

"Victoria or Marble Arch?" he asked politely.

"Charing Cross," she replied with a little laugh.

He watched the cab drive away and then suddenly it stopped, and a figure leant out from the window beckoning him frantically. He ran up to her.

"Suppose I want you?" she asked.

"Advertise," he said promptly, "beginning your advertisement 'Dear Tommy.'"

"I shall put 'TX'," she said indignantly.

"Then I shall take no notice of your advertisement," he replied, and stood in the middle of the street, his hat in his hand, to the intense annoyance of a taxi-cab driver who literally all but ran him down, and in a figurative sense did so until TX was out of earshot.

17

Thomas Xavier Meredith was a shrewd young man. It was said of him by Signor Paulo Coselli, the eminent criminologist, that he had a gift of intuition which was abnormal. Probably the mystery of the twisted candle was solved by him long before any other person in the world had the dimmest idea that it was capable of solution.

The house in Cadogan Square was still in the hands of the police. To this house, and particularly to Kara's bedroom, TX from time to time repaired, and reproduced as far as possible the conditions which obtained on the night of the murder. He had the same stifling fire, the same locked door. The latch was dropped in its socket, whilst TX with a stop watch in his hand made elaborate calculations and acted certain parts which he did not reveal to a soul.

Three times accompanied by Mansus he went to the house, three times went to the death chamber, and was alone on one occasion for an hour and a half whilst the patient Mansus waited outside. Three times he emerged, looking graver on each occasion, and after the third visit he called into consultation John Lexman.

Lexman had been spending some time in the country, having deferred his trip to the United States.

"This case puzzles me more and more, John," said TX, troubled out of his usual boisterous self, "and thank heaven it worries other people besides me. De Mainau came over from France the other day and brought all his best sleuths, whilst O'Grady of the New York central office paid a flying visit just to get hold of the facts. Not one of them has given me the real solution, though they've all been rather ingenious. Gathercole has vanished, and is probably on his way to some undiscoverable region, and our people have not yet traced the valet."

"He should be the easiest for you," said John Lexman reflectively.

"Why Gathercole should go off I can't understand," TX continued. "According to the story which was told me by Fisher, his last words to Kara were to the effect that he was expecting a cheque, or that he had received a cheque. No cheque has been presented or drawn, and apparently Gathercole has gone off without waiting for any payment. An examination of Kara's books shows nothing against the Gathercole account save the sum of £600 which was originally advanced, and now, to upset all my calculations, look at this."

He took from his pocket-book a newspaper cutting and pushed it across the table, for they were dining together at the Carlton. John Lexman picked up the slip and read. It was evidently from a New York paper: "Further news has now come to hand, by the Antarctic Trading Company's steamer *Cyprus*, concerning the wreck of the *City of the Argentine*. It is believed that this ill-fated vessel, which called at South American ports, lost her propeller and drifted south out of the track of shipping. This theory is now confirmed. Apparently the ship struck an iceberg on December 23rd, and foundered with all aboard save a few men who were able to launch a boat, and who were picked up by the *Cyprus*. The following is the passenger list."

John Lexman ran down the list until he came upon a name which was evidently underlined in ink by TX. That name was George Gathercole, and after it in brackets [Explorer].

"If that were true then Gathercole could not have come to London."

"He may have taken another boat," said TX, "and I cabled to the Steamship Company without any great success. Apparently Gathercole was an eccentric sort of man, and lived in terror of being overcrowded. It was a habit of his to make provisional bookings by every available steamer. The company can tell me no more than that he had booked, but whether he shipped on the *City of the Argentine* or not, they do not know."

"I can tell you this about Gathercole," said John slowly and thoughtfully, "that he was a man who would not hurt a fly. He carried his principles to such an extent that he was a vegetarian."

"If you want to sympathise with anybody," said TX gloomily, "sympathise with me."

On the following day TX was summoned to the Home Office, and went steeled for a most unholy row. The Home Secretary, a large and worthy gentleman, given to the making of speeches on every excuse, received him, however, with unusual kindness.

"I've sent for you, Mr Meredith," he said, "about this unfortunate Greek. I've had all his private papers looked into and translated, and in some cases decoded, because, as you are probably aware, his diaries and a great deal of his correspondence were in a code which called for the attention of experts."

TX had not troubled himself greatly about Kara's private papers, but had handed them over, in accordance with instructions, to the proper authorities.

"Of course, Mr Meredith," the Home Secretary went on, beaming across his big table, "we expect you to continue your search for the murderer, but I must confess that your prisoner when you secure him will have a very excellent case to put to a jury."

"That I can well believe, sir," said TX.

"Seldom in my long career at the bar," began the Home Secretary in his best oratorial manner, "have I examined a record so utterly discreditable as that of the deceased man."

Here he advanced a few instances which surprised even TX.

"The man was a lunatic," continued the Home Secretary, "a vicious, evil man who loved cruelty for cruelty's sake. We have in this diary alone sufficient evidence to convict him of three separate murders, one of which was committed in this country."

TX looked his astonishment.

"You will remember, Mr Meredith, as I saw in one of your reports, that he had a chauffeur, a Greek, named Poropolus."

TX nodded.

"He went to Greece on the day following the shooting of Vassalaro," he said.

The Home Secretary shook his head.

"He was killed on the same night," said the Minister, "and you will have no difficulty in finding what remains of his body in the disused house which Kara rented for his own purpose on the Portsmouth Road. That he has killed a number of people in Albania you may well suppose. Whole villages have been wiped out to provide him with a little excitement. The man was Nero without many of Nero's amiable weaknesses. He was obsessed with the idea that he himself was in danger of assassination, and saw an enemy even in his trusty servant. Undoubtedly the chauffeur Poropolus was in touch with several Continental Government circles. You understand," said the Minister in conclusion, "that I am telling you this not with the idea of expecting you to relax your efforts to find the murderer and clear up the mystery, but in order that you may know something of the possible motive for this man's murder."

TX spent an hour going over the decoded diary and documents, and left the Home Office a little shakily. It was inconceivable, incredible. Kara was a lunatic, but the directing genius was a devil.

TX had a flat in Whitehall Gardens, and thither he repaired to change for dinner. He was half dressed when the evening paper arrived, and he glanced, as was his wont, first at the news page and then at the advertisement column. He looked down the column marked "Personal" without expecting to find anything of particular interest to himself, but saw that which made him drop the paper and fly round the room in a frenzy to complete his toilet.

"Tommy X," ran the brief announcement, "most urgent, Marble Arch 8."

He had five minutes to get there, but it seemed like five hours. He was held up at almost every crossing, and though he might have used his authority to obtain right of way, it was a step which his curious sense of honesty prevented him taking. He leapt out of the cab before it stopped, thrust the fare into the driver's hands, and looked round for the girl. He saw her at last and walked quickly towards her. As he approached her she turned about, and with an almost imperceptibly beckoning gesture walked away. He followed her along the Bayswater Road, and gradually drew level.

"I am afraid I have been watched," she said in a low voice; "will you call a cab?"

He hailed a passing taxi, helped her in, and gave at random the first place that suggested itself to him, which was Finsbury Park.

"I am very worried," she said, "and I don't know anybody who can help me except you."

"Is it money?" he asked.

"Money!" she said scornfully, "of course it isn't money! I want to show you a letter," she said after a while.

She took it from her bag and gave it to him, and he struck a match and read it with difficulty.

It was written in a studiously uneducated hand.

Dear Miss,

I know who you are. You are wanted by the police, but I will not give you away. Dear Miss, I am very hard up and £20 will be very useful to me and I shall not trouble you again. Dear Miss, put the money on the window-sill of your room. I know you sleep on the ground floor, and I will come in and take it. And if not – well, I don't want to make any trouble.

Yours truly,
A Friend.

"When did you get this?" he asked.

"This morning," she replied. "I sent the Agony to the paper by telegram, I knew you would come."

"Oh, you did, did you?" he said.

Her assurance was very pleasing to him. The faith that her words implied gave him an odd little feeling of comfort and happiness.

"I can easily get you out of this," he added. "Give me your address, and when the gentleman comes – "

"That is impossible," she replied hurriedly. "Please don't think I'm ungrateful, and don't think I'm being silly. You do think I'm being silly, don't you?"

"I have never harboured such an unworthy thought," he said virtuously.

"Yes, you have," she persisted; "but really I can't tell you where I am living. I have a very special reason for not doing so. It's not myself that I'm thinking about, but there's a life involved."

This was a somewhat dramatic statement to make, and she felt she had gone too far.

"Perhaps I don't mean that," she said, "but there is someone I care for – " She dropped her voice.

"Oh," said TX blankly.

He came down from his rosy heights into the shadow and darkness of a sunless valley.

"Someone you care for," he repeated after a while.

"Yes."

There was another long silence, then: "Oh, indeed," said TX.

Again the unbroken interval of quiet, and after a while she said in a low voice, "Not that way."

"Not what way?" asked TX huskily, his spirits doing a little mountaineering.

"The way you mean," she said.

"Oh," said TX.

He was back again amidst the rosy snows of dawn – was, in fact, climbing a dizzy escalier on the topmost height of hope's Mont Blanc when she pulled the ladder from under him.

"I shall, of course, never marry," she said with a certain prim decision.

TX fell with a dull sickening thud, discovering that his rosy snows were not unlike cold, hard ice in their lack of resilience.

"Who said you would?" he asked somewhat feebly, but in self-defence.

"You did," she said, and her audacity took his breath away.

"Well, how am I to help you?" he asked after a while.

"By giving me some advice," she said. "Do you think I ought to put the money there?"

"Indeed I do not," said TX, recovering some of his natural dominance. "Apart from the fact that you would be compounding a felony, you would merely be laying out trouble for yourself in the future. If he can get £20 so easily, he will come for £40. But why do you stay away? Why don't you return home? There's no charge and no breath of suspicion against you."

"Because I have something to do which I have set my mind to," she said with determination in her tones.

"Surely you can trust me with your address," he urged her, "after all that has passed between us, Belinda Mary – after all the years we have known one another."

"I shall get out and leave you," she said steadily.

"But how the dickens am I going to help you?" he protested.

"Don't swear!" She could be very severe indeed. "The only way you can help me is by being kind and sympathetic."

"Would you like me to burst into tears?" he asked sarcastically.

"I ask you to do nothing more painful or repugnant to your natural feelings than to be a gentleman," she said.

"Thank you very kindly," said TX, and leant back in the cab with an air of supreme resignation.

"I believe you're making faces in the dark," she accused him.

"God forbid that I should do anything so low," said he hastily. "What made you think that?"

"Because I was putting my tongue out at you," she admitted; and the taxi-driver heard the shrieks of laughter in the cab behind him above the wheezing of his asthmatic engine.

At twelve that night in a certain suburb of London an overcoated man moved stealthily through a garden. He felt his way carefully along the wall of the house, and groped with hope, but with no great certainty, along the window-sill. He found an envelope which his fingers, somewhat sensitive from long employment in nefarious uses, told him contained nothing more substantial than a letter.

He went back through the garden and rejoined his companion, who was waiting under an adjacent lamp-post.

"Did she drop?" asked the other eagerly.

"I don't know yet," growled the man from the garden. He opened the envelope and read the few lines.

"She hasn't got the money," he said, "but she's going to get it. I must meet her tomorrow afternoon at the corner of Oxford Street and Regent Street."

"What time?" asked the other.

"Six o'clock," said the first man. "The chap who takes the money must carry a copy of the *Westminster Gazette* in his hand."

"Oh, then it's a plant," said the other with conviction.

The other laughed.

"She won't work any plants. I bet she's scared out of her life."

The second man bit his nails and looked up and down the road apprehensively.

"It's come to something," he said bitterly. "We went out to make our thousands, and we've come down to 'chanting' for £20."

"It's the luck," said the other philosophically, "and I haven't done with her by any means Besides, we've still got a chance of pulling off the big thing, Harry. I reckon she's good for a hundred or two, anyway."

At six o'clock on the following afternoon a man dressed in a dark overcoat, with a soft felt hat pulled down over his eyes, stood nonchalantly by the kerb near where the buses stop at Regent Street slapping his hand gently with a folded copy of the *Westminster Gazette*.

That none should mistake his Liberal reading, he stood as near as possible to a street lamp, and so arranged himself and his attitude that the minimum of light should fall upon his face and the maximum upon that respectable organ of public opinion. Soon after six he saw the girl approaching out of the tail of his eye and strolled off to meet her. To his surprise she passed him by, and he was turning to follow when an unfriendly hand gripped him by the arm.

"Mr Fisher, I believe," said a pleasant voice.

"What do you mean?" said the man, struggling backward.

"Are you going quietly?" asked the pleasant Superintendent Mansus, "or shall I take my stick to you?"

Mr Fisher thought a while.

"It's a cop," he confessed, and allowed himself to be hustled into the waiting cab.

He made his appearance in TX's office, and that urbane gentleman greeted him as a friend.

"And how's Mr Fisher?" he asked. "I suppose you are Mr Fisher still and not Mr Harry Gilcott, or Mr George Porten."

Fisher smiled his old deferential, deprecating smile.

"You will always have your joke, sir. I suppose the young lady gave me away."

"You gave yourself away, my poor Fisher," said TX, and put a strip of paper before him; "you may disguise your hand and in your extreme modesty pretend to an ignorance of the British language which is not creditable to your many attainments, but what you must be awfully careful in doing in future when you write such epistles," he said, "is to wash your hands."

"Wash my hands?" repeated the puzzled Fisher.

TX nodded.

"You see you left a little thumb print and we are rather whales on thumb prints at Scotland Yard, Fisher."

"I see. What is the charge now, sir?"

"I shall make no charge against you except the conventional one of being a convict under licence and failing to report."

Fisher heaved a sigh.

"That'll only mean twelve months. Are you going to charge me with this business?" He nodded to the paper.

TX shook his head.

"I bear you no ill-will, although you tried to frighten Miss Bartholomew. Oh yes, I know it is Miss Bartholomew, and have known all the time. The lady is there for a reason which is no business of yours or of mine. I shall not charge you with attempt to blackmail, and in reward for my leniency I hope you are going to tell me all you know about the Kara murder. You wouldn't like me to charge you with that, would you, by any chance?"

Fisher drew a long breath.

"No, sir; but if you did I could prove my innocence," he said earnestly. "I spent the whole of the evening in the kitchen."

"Except a quarter of an hour," said TX.

The man nodded.

"That's true, sir, I went out to see a pal of mine."

"The man who is in this?" asked TX.

Fisher hesitated.

"Yes, sir. He was with me in this, but there was nothing wrong about the business – as far as we went. I don't mind admitting that I was planning a Big Thing. I'm not going to blow on it, if it's going to get me into trouble, but if you'll promise me that it won't, I'll tell you the whole story."

"Against whom was this coup of yours planned?"

"Against Mr Kara, sir," said Fisher.

"Go on with your story," nodded TX.

The story was a short and commonplace one. Fisher had met a man who knew another man who was either a Turk or an Albanian. They had learnt that Kara was in the habit of keeping large sums of money in the house, and they had planned to rob him. That was the story in a nutshell. Somewhere the plan miscarried. It was when he came to the incidents that occurred on the night of the murder that TX followed him with the greatest interest.

"The old gentleman came in," said Fisher, "and I saw him up to the room. I heard him coming out, and I went up and spoke to him while he was having a chat with Mr Kara at the open door."

"Did you hear Mr Kara speak?"

"I fancy I did, sir," said Fisher, "anyway the old gentleman was quite pleased with himself."

"Why do you say 'old gentleman?' " asked TX, "he was not an old man."

"Not exactly, sir," said Fisher, "but he had a sort of fussy, irritable way that old gentlemen sometimes have, and I somehow got it fixed in my mind that he was old. As a matter of fact he was about forty-five, he may have been fifty."

"You have told me all this before. Was there anything peculiar about him?"

Fisher hesitated.

"Nothing, sir, except the fact that one of his arms was a game one."

"Meaning that it was — "

"Meaning that it was an artificial one, sir, so far as I can make out."

"Was it his right or his left arm that was game?" interrupted TX.

"His left arm, sir."

"You're sure?"

"I'd swear to it, sir."

"Very well, go on."

"He came downstairs and went out, and I never saw him again. When you came and the murder was discovered, and knowing as I did that I had my own scheme on and that one of your splits might pinch me, I got a bit rattled. I went downstairs to the hall and the first thing I saw lying on the table was a letter. It was addressed to me."

He paused, and TX nodded.

"Go on," he said again.

"I couldn't understand how it came to be there, but as I'd been in the kitchen most of the evening, except when I was seeing my pal outside to tell him the job was off for that night, it might have been there before you came. I opened the letter. There were only a few words in it, and I can tell you those few words made my heart jump up into my mouth, and made me go cold all over."

"What were they?" asked TX.

"I shall not forget them, sir. They're sort of permanently fixed in my brain," said the man earnestly. "The note started with just the figures 'AC 274.' "

"What was that?" asked TX.

"My convict number when I was in Dartmoor Prison, sir."

"What did the note say?"

" 'Get out of here, quick' – I don't know who had put it there, but I'd evidently been spotted, and I was taking no chances. That's the whole story from beginning to end. I accidentally happened to meet the young lady, Miss Holland – Miss Bartholomew as she is – and followed her to her house in Portman Place. That was the night you were there."

TX found himself to his intense annoyance going very red.

"And you know no more?" he asked.

"No more, sir."

"There is one thing I would like to ask you," said the girl when he met her next morning in Green Park. "If you were going to ask whether I made inquiries as to where your habitation was," he warned her, "I beg of you to refrain."

She was looking radiantly beautiful that morning, he thought. The keen air had brought a colour to her face and lent a spring to her gait, and as she strode along by his side with the free and careless swing of youth, she was an epitome of the life which even now was budding on every tree in the park.

"Your father is back in town, by the way," he said, "and he is most anxious to see you."

She made a little grimace. "I hope you haven't been round talking to father about me."

"Of course I have," he said helplessly. "I have also had all the reporters up from Fleet Street, and given them a full description of your escapades."

She looked round at him with laughter in her eyes.

"You have all the manners of an early Christian martyr," she said. "Poor soul! Would you like to be thrown to the lions?"

"I should prefer being thrown to the demnition ducks and drakes," he said moodily.

"You're such a miserable man," she chided him, "and yet you have everything to make life worth living."

"Ha ha," said TX.

"You have; of course you have! You have a splendid position. Everybody looks up to you and talks about you. You have got a wife and family who adore you – "

He stopped and looked at her as though she were some strange insect.

"I have a how much?" he asked credulously.

"Aren't you married?" she asked innocently.

He made a strange noise in his throat.

"Do you know I have always thought of you as married," she went on. "I often picture you in your domestic circle reading to the children from the *Daily Megaphone* those awfully interesting stories about Little Willie Waterbug."

He held on to the railings for support. "May we sit down?" he asked faintly.

She sat by his side, half turned to him, demure and wholly adorable.

"Of course you are right in one respect," he said at last, "but you're altogether wrong about the children."

"Are you married?" she demanded with no evidence of amusement.

"Didn't you know?" he asked.

She swallowed something. "Of course it's no business of mine, and I'm sure I hope you are very happy."

"Perfectly happy," said TX complacently. "You must come and see me one Saturday afternoon when I am digging the potatoes. I am a perfect devil when they let me loose in the vegetable garden."

"Shall we go on?" she said.

He could have sworn there were tears in her eyes, and manlike he thought she was vexed with him at his fooling.

"I haven't made you cross, have I?" he asked.

"Oh no," she replied.

"I mean you don't believe all this rot about my being married and that sort of thing."

"I'm not interested," she said with a shrug of her shoulders, "not very much. You've been very kind to me and I should be an awful boor if I wasn't grateful. Of course, I don't care whether you're married or not, it's nothing to do with me, is it?"

"Naturally it isn't," he replied. "I suppose you aren't married by any chance?"

"Married," she repeated bitterly, "why you will make my fourth!"

She had hardly got the words out of her mouth before she realised her terrible error. A second later she was in his arms and he was kissing her, to the scandal of one aged parkkeeper, one small and dirty-faced little boy, and a moulting duck who seemed to sneer at the proceedings which he watched through a yellow and malignant eye.

"Belinda Mary," said TX at parting, "you have got to give up your little country establishment wherever it may be and come back to the discomforts of Portman Place. Oh, I know you can't come back yet. That somebody is there, and I can pretty well guess who it is?"

"Who?" she challenged.

"I rather fancy your mother has come back," he suggested.

A look of scorn dawned into her pretty face.

"Good Lord, Tommy!" she said in disgust, "you don't think I should keep mother in the suburbs without her telling the world all about it?"

"You're an undutiful little beggar," he said.

They had reached the Horse Guards at Whitehall, and he was saying goodbye to her.

"If it comes to a matter of duty," she answered, "perhaps you will do your duty and hold up the traffic for me and let me cross this road."

"My dear girl," he protested, "hold up the traffic?"

"Of course," she said indignantly, "you're a policeman."

"Only when I am in uniform," he said hastily, and piloted her across the road.

It was a new man who returned to the gloomy office in Whitehall – a man with a heart that swelled and throbbed with the pride and joy of life's most precious possession.

18

TX sat at his desk, his chin in his hands, his mind remarkably busy. Grave as the matter was which he was considering, he rose with alacrity to meet the smiling girl who was ushered through the door by Mansus preternaturally solemn and mysterious.

She was radiant that day. Her eyes were sparkling with an unusual brightness.

"I've got the most wonderful thing to tell you," she said, "and I can't tell you."

"That's a very good beginning," said TX, taking her muff from her hand.

"Oh, but it's really wonderful," she cried eagerly, "more wonderful than anything you have ever heard about."

"We are interested," said TX blandly.

"No, no, you mustn't make fun," she begged. "I can't tell you now, but it is something that will make you simply – " she was at a loss for a simile.

"Jump out of my skin?" suggested TX.

"I will astonish you." She nodded her head solemnly.

"I take a lot of astonishing, I warn you," he smiled. "To know you is to exhaust one's capacity for surprise."

"That can be either very, very nice or very, very nasty," she said cautiously.

"But accept it as being very, very nice," he laughed. "Now come, out with this tale of yours!"

She shook her head very vigorously.

"I can't possibly tell you anything," she said.

143

"Then why the dickens do you begin telling anything for?" he complained, not without reason.

"Because I just want you to know that I *do* know something."

"Oh Lord," he groaned, "of course you know everything. Belinda Mary, you're really the most wonderful child."

He sat on the edge of the armchair and laid his hand on her shoulder.

"And you've come to take me out to lunch?"

"What were you worrying about when I came in?" she asked.

"Nothing very much. You've heard me speak of John Lexman?"

She nodded, and again TX noticed the suppressed eagerness in her eyes.

"You're not ill or sickening for anything, are you?" he asked anxiously.

"Don't be silly," she said, "go on and tell me something about Mr Lexman."

"He's going to America," said TX, "and before he goes he wants to give a little lecture."

"A lecture?"

"It sounds rum, doesn't it? But that's just what he wants to do."

"Why is he doing it?" she asked.

TX made a gesture of despair.

"That is one of the mysteries which may never be revealed to me, except – " He pursed his lips and looked thoughtfully at the girl. "There are times," he said, "when there is a great struggle going on inside a man between all the human and better part of him and the baser professional part of him. One side of me wants to hear this lecture of John Lexman's very much, the other shrinks from the ordeal."

"Let us talk it over at lunch," she said practically, and carried him off.

19

One would not readily associate the party of top-booted sewer-men who descend nightly to the subterranean passages of London with the stout vice-consul at Durazzo. Yet it was one unimaginative man who lived in Lambeth and had no knowledge that there was such a place as Durazzo who was responsible for bringing this comfortable official out of his bed in the early hours of the morning and caused him – albeit reluctantly and with violent and insubordinate language – to conduct certain investigations in the crowded bazaars.

At first he was unsuccessful because there were many Hussein Effendis in Durazzo. He sent an invitation to the American Consul to come over to tiffin and help him.

"Why the dickens the Foreign Office should suddenly be interested in Hussein Effendi I cannot for the life of me understand."

"The Foreign Department has to be interested in something, you know," said the genial American. "I receive some of the quaintest requests from Washington. I rather fancy they only wire you to find if you are there. Why are you doing this?"

"I've seen Hakaat Bey," said the English official. "I wonder what this fellow has been doing? There is probably a wigging for me in the offing."

At about the same time the sewer-man in the bosom of his own family was taking loud and noisy sips from a big mug of tea.

"Don't you be surprised," he said to his admiring better half, "if I have to go up to the Old Bailey to give evidence."

"Lord, Joe!" she said with interest, "what has happened?"

The sewer-man filled his pipe and told the story with a wealth of rambling detail. He gave particulars of the hour he had descended the Victoria Street shaft, of what Bill Morgan had said to him as they were going down, of what he had said to Harry Carter as they splashed along the low-roofed tunnel, of how he had a funny feeling that he was going to make a discovery, and so on and so forth until he reached his long-delayed climax.

TX waited up very late that night, and at twelve o'clock his patience was rewarded, for the Foreign Office messenger brought a telegram to him. It was addressed to the Chief Secretary and ran:

> No. 847. Yours 63952 of yesterday's date. Begins. Hussein Effendi a prosperous merchant of this city left for Italy to place his daughter in convent Marie Theressa Florence Hussein being Christian. He goes on to Paris. Apply Ralli Theokritis et Cie, Rue de l'Opéra. Ends.

Half-an-hour later TX had a telephone connection through to Paris, and was instructing the British police agent in that city. He received a further telephone report from Paris the next morning, and one which gave him infinite satisfaction. Very slowly but surely he was gathering together the pieces of this baffling mystery, and was fitting them together. Hussein Effendi would probably supply the last missing segments.

At eight o'clock that night the door opened, and the man who represented TX in Paris came in carrying a travelling ulster on his arm. TX gave him a nod, and then as the newcomer stood with the door open obviously waiting for somebody to follow him, he said: "Show him in – I will see him alone."

There walked into his office a tall man wearing a frock-coat and a red fez. He was a man of from fifty-five to sixty, powerfully built, with a grave dark face and a thin fringe of white beard. He salaamed as he entered.

"You speak French, I believe," said TX presently.

The other bowed.

"My agent has explained to you," said TX in French, "that I desire some information for the purpose of clearing up a crime which has been committed in this country. I have given you my assurance, if that assurance was necessary, that you would come to no harm as a result of anything you might tell me."

"That I understand, Effendi," said the tall Turk; "the Americans and the English have always been good friends of mine, and I have been frequently in London. Therefore, I shall be very pleased to be of any help to you."

TX walked to a closed bookcase on one side of the room, unlocked it, took out an object wrapped in white tissue-paper. He laid this on the table, the Turk watching the proceedings with an impassive face. Very slowly the Commissioner unrolled the little bundle, and revealed at last a long slim knife, rusted and stained with a hilt which in its untarnished days had evidently been of chased silver. He lifted the dagger from the table and handed it to the Turk.

"This is yours, I believe," he said softly.

The man turned it over, stepping nearer the table that he might secure the advantage of a better light. He examined the blade near the hilt and handed the weapon back to TX.

"That is my knife," he said.

TX smiled.

"You understand, of course, that I saw 'Hussein Effendi of Durazzo' inscribed in Arabic near the hilt."

The Turk inclined his head.

"With this weapon," TX went on, speaking with slow emphasis, "a murder was committed in this town."

There was no sign of interest or astonishment, or indeed of any emotion whatever.

"It is the will of God," he said calmly, "these things happen even in a great city like London."

"It was your knife," suggested TX.

"But my hand was in Durazzo, Effendi," said the Turk.

He looked at the knife again.

147

"So the Black Roman is dead, Effendi."

"The Black Roman?" asked TX, a little puzzled.

"The Greek they call Kara," said the Turk, "he was a very wicked man."

TX was up on his feet now, leaning across the table and looking at the other with narrowed eyes.

"How did you know it was Kara?" he asked quickly.

The Turk shrugged his shoulders.

"Who else could it be?" he said, "are not your newspapers filled with the story?"

TX sat back again, disappointed and a little angry with himself.

"That is true, Hussein Effendi, but I did not think you read the papers."

"Neither do I, master," replied the other coolly, "nor did I know that Kara had been killed until I saw this knife. How came this in your possession?"

"It was found in a rain sewer," said TX, "into which the murderer had apparently dropped it. But if you have not read the newspapers, Effendi, then you admit that you know who committed this murder."

The Turk raised his hands slowly to a level with his shoulders.

"Though I am a Christian," he said, "there are many wise sayings of my father's religion which I remember. And one of these, Effendi, was, 'the wicked must die in the habitations of the just; by the weapons of the worthy shall the wicked perish.' Your Excellency, I am a worthy man, for never have I done a dishonest thing in my life. I have traded fairly with Greeks, with Italians, with Frenchmen, and with Englishmen, also with Jews. I have never sought to rob them nor to hurt them. If I have killed men, God knows it was not because I desired their death, but because their lives were dangerous to me and to mine. Ask the blade all your questions and see what answer it gives. Until it speaks I am as dumb as the blade, for it is also written that 'the soldier is the servant of his sword,' and also 'the wise servant is dumb about his master's affairs.'"

TX laughed helplessly.

"I had hoped that you might be able to help me – hoped and feared," he said; "if you cannot speak it is not my business to force you either by threat or by act. I am grateful to you for having come over, although the visit has been rather fruitless so far as I am concerned."

He smiled again and offered his hand.

"Excellency," said the old Turk soberly, "there are some things in life that are well left alone, and there are moments when justice should be so blind that she does not see guilt – here is such a moment."

And this ended the interview, one on which TX had set very high hopes. His gloom carried to Portman Place where he had arranged to meet Belinda Mary.

"Where is Mr Lexman going to give this famous lecture of his?" was the question with which she greeted him, "and please, what is the subject?"

"It is on a subject which is of supreme interest to me," he said gravely; "he has called his lecture 'The Clue of the Twisted Candle.' There is no clearer brain being employed in the business of criminal detection than John Lexman's. Though he uses his genius for the construction of stories, were it employed in the legitimate business of police work, I am certain he would make a mark second to none in the world. He is determined on giving this lecture, and he has issued a number of invitations. These include the Chiefs of the Secret Police of nearly all the civilised countries of the world. O'Grady is on his way from America, he wirelessed me this morning to that effect. Even the Chief of the Russian police has accepted the invitation, because as you know this murder has excited a great deal of interest in police circles everywhere. John Lexman is not only going to deliver this lecture," he said slowly, "but he is going to tell us who committed the murder and how it was committed."

She thought a moment.

"Where will it be delivered?"

"I don't know," he said in astonishment, "does that matter?"

"It matters a great deal," she said emphatically, "especially if I want it delivered in a certain place. Would you induce Mr Lexman to lecture at my house?"

"At Portman Place?" he asked.

She shook her head.

"No, I have a house of my own. A furnished house I have rented at Blackheath. Will you induce Mr Lexman to give the lecture there?"

"But why?" he asked.

"Please don't ask questions," she pleaded; "do this for me, Tommy."

He saw she was in earnest.

"I'll write to old Lexman this afternoon," he promised.

John Lexman telephoned his reply.

"I should prefer somewhere out of London," he said, "and since Miss Bartholomew has some interest in the matter, may I extend my invitation to her? – I promise she shall not be any more shocked than a good woman need be."

And so it came about that the name of Belinda Mary Bartholomew was added to the selected list of police chiefs who were making for London at that moment to hear from the man who had guaranteed the solution, the story of Kara and his killing and the unravelment of the mystery which surrounded his death, and the significance of the twisted candles, which at that moment were reposing in the Black Museum at Scotland Yard.

20

The room was a big one and most of the furniture had been cleared out to admit the guests who had come from the ends of the earth to learn the story of the twisted candles, and to test John Lexman's theory by their own.

They sat around chatting cheerfully of men and crimes, of great coups planned and frustrated, of strange deeds committed and undetected. Scraps of their conversation came to Belinda Mary as she stood in the chintz-draped doorway which led from the drawing-room to the room she used as a study.

"...do you remember, Sir George, the Bolbrook case? I took the man at Odessa..."

"...the curious thing was that I found no money on the body, only a small gold charm set with a single emerald, so I *knew* it was the girl with the fur bonnet who had..."

"...Pinot got away after putting three bullets into me, but I dragged myself to the window and shot him dead – it was a real good shot..."

They rose to meet her and TX introduced her to the men. It was at that moment that John Lexman was announced.

He looked tired, but returned the Commissioner's greeting with a cheerful mien. He knew all the men present by name as they knew him. He had a few sheets of notes which he laid on the little table which had been placed for him, and when the introductions were finished he went to this and with scarcely any preliminary began –

21

(The narrative of John Lexman)

"I am, as you may all know, a writer of stories which depend for their success upon the creation and unravelment of criminological mysteries. The Chief Commissioner has been good enough to tell you that my stories were something more than a mere seeking after sensation, and that I endeavoured in the course of those narratives to propound obscure but possible situations, and with the ingenuity that I could command to offer to those problems a solution acceptable not only to the general reader but to the police expert.

"Although I did not regard my earlier work with any great seriousness and, indeed, only sought after exciting situations and incidents, I can see now, looking back, that underneath the work which seemed at the time purposeless, there was something very much like a scheme of studies.

"You must forgive this egotism in me because it is necessary that I should make this explanation, and you, who are in the main police officers of considerable experience and discernment, should appreciate the fact that as I was able to get inside the minds of the fictitious criminals I portrayed, so am I now able to follow the mind of the man who committed this murder, or if not follow his mind, I may recreate the psychology of the slayer of Remington Kara.

"In the possession of most of you are the vital facts concerning this man. You know the type of man he was, you have instances of his terrible ruthlessness, you know that he was a blot upon God's earth, a vicious ego seeking the gratification of that strange blood lust and pain lust which is to be found in so few criminals."

John Lexman went on to describe the killing of Vassalaro.

"I know now how that occurred," he said. "I had received on the previous Christmas Eve, amongst other presents, a pistol from an unknown admirer. That unknown admirer was Kara, who had planned this murder some three months ahead. He it was who sent me the Browning, knowing as he did that I had never used such a weapon, and that therefore I would be chary about using it. I might have put the pistol away in a cupboard out of reach and the whole of his carefully thought out plan would have miscarried.

"But Kara was systematic in all things. Three weeks after I received the weapon a clumsy attempt was made to break into my house in the middle of the night. It struck me at the time it was clumsy, because the burglar made a tremendous amount of noise and disappeared soon after he began his attempt, doing no more damage than to break a window in my dining-room. Naturally my mind went to the possibility of a further attempt of this kind, as my house stood on the outskirts of the village, and it was only natural that I should take the pistol from one of my boxes and put it somewhere handy. To make doubly sure Kara came down the next day and heard the full story of the outrage.

"He did not speak of pistols, but I remember now, though I did not remember at the time, that I mentioned the fact that I had a handy weapon. A fortnight later a second attempt was made to enter the house. I say an attempt, but again I do not believe that the intention was at all serious. The outrage was designed to keep that pistol of mine in a get-at-able place.

"And again Kara came down to see us on the day following the attempted burglary, and again I must have told him, though I have no distinct recollection of the fact, of what had happened the previous night. It would have been unnatural if I had not mentioned the fact, as it was a matter which had formed a subject of discussion between myself, my wife, and the servants.

"Then came the threatening letter with Kara providentially at hand. On the night of the murder, whilst Kara was still in my house, I went out to find his chauffeur. He remained a few minutes with my wife and then on some excuse went into the library. There he loaded the pistol, placing one cartridge in the chamber and trusting to luck that I did not pull the trigger until I had it pointed at my victim. Here he took his biggest chance, because before sending the weapon to me, he had had the spring of the Browning so eased that the slightest touch set it off, and, as you know, the pistol being automatic, the explosion of one cartridge reloading and firing the next and so on, it was probable that a chance touch would have brought his scheme to naught – probably me also.

"Of what happened on that night you are aware."

He went on to tell of his trial and conviction and skimmed over the life he led until that morning on Dartmoor.

"Kara knew my innocence had been proved, and his hatred for me being his great obsession since I had the thing he had wanted – but no longer wanted, let that be understood – he saw the misery he had planned for me and my dear wife being brought to a sudden end. He had, by the way, already planned and carried his plan into execution, a system of tormenting her.

"You did not know," he turned to TX, "that scarcely a month passed but some disreputable villain called at her flat, with a story that he had been released from Portland or Wormwood Scrubs that morning and that he had seen me. The story each messenger brought was one sufficient to break the heart of any but the bravest woman. It was a story of ill-treatment by brutal officials, of my illness, of my madness, of everything calculated to harrow the feelings of a tender-hearted and faithful wife.

"That was Kara's scheme. Not to hurt with the whip or with the knife, but to cut deep at the heart with his evil tongue, to cut to the raw places of the mind. When he found that I was to be released – he may have guessed, or he may have discovered by some underhand method, that a pardon was about to be signed – he conceived his great plan. He had less than two days to execute it.

"Through one of his agents he discovered a warder who had been in some trouble with the authorities, a man who was avaricious and was even then on the brink of being discharged from the service for trafficking with prisoners. The bribe he offered this man was a heavy one and the warder accepted.

"Kara had purchased a monoplane, and, as you know, he was an excellent aviator. With this new machine he flew to Devon and arrived at dawn in one of the unfrequented parts of the moor.

"The story of my own escape needs no telling. My narrative really begins from the moment I put my foot upon the deck of the *Mpret*. The first person I asked to see was, naturally, my wife. Kara, however, insisted on my going to the cabin he had prepared and changing my clothes, and until then I did not realise I was still in my convict's garb. A clean change was waiting for me, and the luxury of soft shirts and well-fitting garments after the prison uniform I cannot describe.

"After I was dressed I was taken by the Greek steward to the larger state-room, and there I found my darling waiting for me."

His voice sank almost to a whisper, and it was a minute or two before he had mastered his emotion.

"She had been suspicious of Kara, but he had been very insistent. He had detailed the plans and shown her the monoplane, but even then she would not trust herself on board, and she had been waiting in a motor-boat moving parallel with the yacht until she saw the landing and realised, as she thought, that Kara was not playing her false. The motor-boat had been hired by Kara, and the two men inside were probably as well bribed as the warder.

"The joy of freedom can only be known to those who have suffered the horrors of restraint. That is a trite enough statement, but when one is describing elemental things there is no room for subtlety. The voyage was a fairly eventless one. We saw very little of Kara, who did not intrude himself upon us, and our main excitement lay in the apprehension that we should be held up by a British destroyer, or that when we reached Gibraltar we should be searched by the British authorities. Kara had foreseen that possibility and had taken in enough coal to last him for the run.

"We had a fairly stormy passage in the Mediterranean, but after that nothing happened until we arrived at Durazzo. We had to go ashore in disguise because Kara told us that the English Consul might see us and make some trouble. We wore Turkish dresses, Grace heavily veiled, and I wearing a greasy old kaftan, which with my somewhat emaciated face and my unshaven appearance passed me without comment.

"Kara's home was, and is, about eighteen miles from Durazzo. It is not on the main road, but it is reached by following one of the rocky mountain paths which wind and twist among the hills to the south-east of the town. The country is wild and mainly uncultivated. We had to pass through swamps and skirt huge lagoons as we mounted higher and higher from terrace to terrace, and came to the mountain roads which crossed the mountains.

"Kara's palace – you could call it no less – is really built within sight of the sea. It is on the Acroceraunian Peninsula near Cape Linguetta. Hereabouts the country is more populated and better cultivated. We passed great slopes entirely covered with mulberry and olive trees, whilst in the valleys there were fields of maize and corn. The palazzo stands on a lofty plateau. It is approached by two paths which can be, and have been, well defended in the past against the Sultan's troops or against the bands which have been raised by rival villages with the object of storming and plundering this stronghold.

"The Skipetars, a bloodthirsty crowd without pity or remorse, were faithful enough to their chief as Kara was. He paid them so well that it was not profitable to rob him; moreover he kept their own turbulent elements fully occupied with the little raids which he or his agents organised from time to time. The palazzo was built rather in the Moorish than in the Turkish style.

"It was partly Eastern in character, to which was grafted an Italian architecture – a house of white-columned courts, of big paved yards, fountains and cool dark rooms.

"When I passed through the gates I realised for the first time something of Kara's importance. There were a score of servants, all

Eastern, perfectly trained, silent and obsequious. He led us to his own room.

"It was a big apartment with divans running round the wall, the most ornate French drawing-room suite and an enormous Persian carpet, one of the finest of the kind that have ever been turned out of Shiraz. Here let me say that throughout the trip his attitude to me had been perfectly friendly, and towards Grace all that I could ask of my best friend, considerate and tactful.

"We had hardly reached his room before he said to me with that *bonhomie* which he had observed throughout the trip, 'You would like to see your room?'

"I expressed a wish to that effect. He clapped his hands and a big Albanian servant came through the curtained doorway, made the usual salaam, and Kara spoke to him a few words in a language which I presume was Turkish.

" 'He will show you the way,' said Kari with his most genial smile.

"I followed the servant through the curtains, which had hardly fallen behind me before I was seized by four men, flung violently on the ground, a filthy tarbosch was thrust into my mouth, and before I knew what was happening I was bound hand and foot.

"As I realised the gross treachery of the man, my first frantic thoughts were of Grace and her safety. I struggled with the strength of three men, but they were too many for me, and I was dragged along the passage, a door was opened, and I was flung into a bare room. I must have been lying on the floor for half an hour when they came for me, this time accompanied by a middle-aged man named Salvolio, who was either an Italian or a Greek.

"He spoke English fairly well, and he made it clear to me that I had to behave myself. I was led back to the room from whence I had come, and found Kara sitting in one of those big armchairs which he affected, smoking a cigarette. Confronting him, still in her Turkish dress, was poor Grace. She was not bound, I was pleased to see, but when on my entrance she rose and made as if to come towards me, she was unceremoniously thrown back by the guardian who stood at her side.

" 'Mr John Lexman,' drawled Kara, 'you are at the beginning of a great disillusionment. I have a few things to tell you which will make you feel rather uncomfortable.' It was then that I heard for the first time that my pardon had been signed and my innocence discovered.

" 'Having taken a great deal of trouble to get you in prison,' said Kara, 'it isn't likely that I'm going to allow all my plans to be undone, and my plan is to make you both extremely uncomfortable.'

"He did not raise his voice, speaking still in the same conversational tone, suave and half amused.

" 'I hate you for two things,' he said, and ticked them off on his fingers; 'the first is that you took the woman I wanted. To a man of my temperament that is an unpardonable crime. I have never wanted women either as friends or as amusement. I am one of the few people in the world who are self-sufficient. It happened that I wanted your wife and she rejected me because apparently she preferred you.'

"He looked at me quizzically. 'You are thinking at this moment,' he went on slowly, 'that I want her now, and that it is part of my revenge that I shall put her straight in my harem. Nothing is farther from my desires or my thoughts. The Black Roman is not satisfied with the leavings of such poor trash as you. I hate you both equally, and for both of you there is waiting an experience more terrible than even your elastic imagination can conjure. You understand what that means?' he asked me, still retaining his calm.

"I did not reply. I dared not look at Grace, to whom he turned.

" 'I believe you love your husband, my friend,' he said; 'your love will be put to a very severe test. You shall see him the mere wreckage of the man he is. You shall see him brutalised below the level of the cattle in the field. I will give you both no joys, no ease of mind. From this moment you are slaves, and worse than slaves.'

"He clapped his hands. The interview was ended, and from that moment I only saw Grace once."

John Lexman stopped and buried his face in his hands.

"They took me to an underground dungeon cut in the solid rock. In many ways it resembled the dungeon of the Château of Chillon, in that its only window looked out upon a wild storm-swept lake, and its floor was jagged rock. I have called it underground as, indeed, it was on that side, for the palazzo was built upon a steep slope running down from the spur of the hills.

"They chained me by the legs and left me to my own devices. Once a day they gave me a little goat-flesh and a pannikin of water, and once a week Kara would come in, and outside the radius of my chain he would open a little camp stool and, sitting down, smoke his cigarette and talk. My God! the things that man said! The things he described! The horrors he related! And always it was Grace who was the centre of his description. And he would relate the stories he was telling to her about myself. I cannot describe them. They are beyond repetition."

John Lexman shuddered and closed his eyes. "That was his weapon. He did not confront me with the torture of my darling, he did not bring tangible evidence of her suffering – he just sat and talked, describing with remarkable clarity of language which seemed incredible in a foreigner, the 'amusements' which he had witnessed.

"I thought I should go mad. Twice I sprang at him and twice the chain about my legs threw me headlong on that cruel floor. Once he brought the gaoler in to whip me, but I took the whipping with such phlegm that it gave him no satisfaction. I told you I had seen Grace only once, and this is how it happened.

"It was after the flogging, and Kara, who was a veritable demon in his rage, planned to have his revenge for my indifference. They brought Grace out upon a boat, and rowed the boat to where I could see it from my window. There the whip which had been applied to me was applied to her. I can't tell you any more about that," he said brokenly, "but I wish, you don't know how fervently, that I had broken down and given the dog the satisfaction he wanted. My God! It was horrible!

"When the winter came they used to take me out with chains upon my legs to gather in wood from the forest. There was no reason why I should be given this work, but the truth was, as I discovered from Salvolio, that Kara thought my dungeon was too warm. It was sheltered from the winds by the hill behind, and even on the coldest days and nights it was not unbearable. Then Kara went away for some time. I think he must have gone to England, and he came back in a white fury. One of his big plans had gone wrong, and the mental torture he inflicted upon me was more acute than ever.

"In the old days he used to come once a week, now he came almost every day. He usually arrived in the afternoon, and I was surprised one night to be awakened from my sleep to see him standing at the door, a lantern in his hand, his inevitable cigarette in his mouth. He always wore the Albanian costume when he was in the country, those white kilted skirts and zouave jackets which the hillsmen affect, and, if anything, it added to his demoniacal appearance. He put down the lantern and leant against the wall.

" 'I'm afraid that wife of yours is breaking up, Lexman,' he drawled; 'she isn't the good stout English stuff that I thought she was.'

"I made no reply. I had found by bitter experience that if I intruded into the conversation, I should only suffer the more.

" 'I have sent down to Durazzo to get a doctor,' he went on. 'Naturally, having taken all this trouble I don't want to lose you by death. She is breaking up,' he repeated with relish, and yet with an undernote of annoyance in his voice; 'she asked for you three times this morning.'

"I kept myself under control as I had never expected that a man so desperately circumstanced could do.

" 'Kara,' I said as quietly as I could, 'what has she done that she should deserve this hell in which she has lived?'

"He sent out a long ring of smoke and watched its progress across the dungeon.

" 'What has she done?' he said, keeping his eye on the ring – I shall always remember every look, every gesture, and every intonation of his voice. 'Why, she has done all that a woman can do for a man like me. She has made me feel little. Until I had a rebuff from her, I had all the world at my feet, Lexman. I did as I liked. If I crooked my little finger, people ran after me, and that one experience with her has broken me. Oh, don't think,' he went on quickly, 'that I am broken in love. I never loved her very much, it was just a passing passion, but she killed my self-confidence. After then, whenever I came to a crucial moment in my affairs, when the big manner, the big certainty was absolutely* necessary for me to carry my way; whenever I was most confident of myself and my ability and my scheme, a vision of this damned girl rose, and I felt that momentary weakening, that memory of defeat, which made all the difference between success and failure.

" 'I hated her and I hate her still,' he said with vehemence; 'if she dies I shall hate her more because she will remain everlastingly unbroken to menace my thoughts and spoil my schemes through all eternity.'

"He leant forward, his elbows on his knees, his clenched fist under his chin – how well I can see him! – and stared at me.

" 'I could have been king here in this land,' he said, waving his hand toward the interior. 'I could have bribed and shot my way to the throne of Albania. Don't you realise what that means to a man like me? There is still a chance; and if I could keep your wife alive – if I could see her broken in reason and in health, a poor skeleton gibbering thing that knelt at my feet when I came near her, I should recover the mastery of myself. Believe me,' he said, nodding his head, 'your wife will have the best medical advice 0it is possible to obtain.'

"Kara went out, and I did not see him again for a very long time. He sent word, just a scrawled note in the morning, to say my wife had died."

John Lexman rose up from his seat and paced the apartment, his head upon his breast.

"From that moment," he said, "I lived only for one thing – to punish Remington Kara. And, gentlemen, I punished him."

He stood in the centre of the room and thumped his broad chest with his clenched hand. "I killed Remington Kara," he said, and there was a little gasp of astonishment from every man present save one.

That one was TX Meredith, who had known all the time.

22

After a while Lexman resumed his story: "I told you that there was a man at the palazzo named Salvolio. Salvolio had been undergoing a life sentence in one of the prisons of southern Italy. In some mysterious fashion he escaped and got across the Adriatic in a small boat. How Kara found him I don't know. Salvolio was a very uncommunicative person. I was never certain whether he was a Greek or an Italian. All that I am sure about is that he was the most unmitigated villain next to his master that I have ever met.

"He was a quick man with his knife, and I have seen him kill one of the guards whom he had thought was favouring me in the matter of diet with less compunction than you would kill a rat.

"It was he who gave me this scar" – John Lexman pointed to his cheek. "In his master's absence he took upon himself the task of conducting a clumsy imitation of Kara's persecution. He gave me, too, the only glimpse I ever had of the torture which poor Grace underwent. She hated dogs, and Kara must have come to know this, and in her sleeping-room – she was apparently better accommodated than I – he kept four fierce beasts so chained that they could almost reach her.

"Some reference to my wife from this low brute maddened me beyond endurance, and I sprang at him. He whipped out his knife and struck at me as I fell, and I escaped by a miracle. He evidently had orders not to touch me, for he was in a great panic of mind, as he had reason to be, because on Kara's return he discovered the state of my face, started an inquiry, and had Salvolio taken to the courtyard in the true Eastern style and bastinadoed until his feet were pulp.

"You may be sure the man hated me with a malignity which almost rivalled his employer's. After Grace's death Kara went away suddenly, and I was left to the tender mercy of this man. Evidently he had been given a fairly free hand. The principal object of Kara's hate being dead, he took little further interest in me, or else wearied of his hobby. Salvolio began his persecutions by reducing my diet. Fortunately I ate very little. Nevertheless the supplies began to grow less and less, and I was beginning to feel the effects of this starvation system when there happened a thing which changed the whole course of my life and opened to me a way to freedom and to vengeance.

"Salvolio did not imitate the austerity of his master, and in Kara's absence was in the habit of having little orgies of his own. He would bring up dancing girls from Durazzo for his amusement, and invite prominent men in the neighbourhood to his feasts and entertainments, for he was absolutely lord of the palazzo when Kara was away, and could do pretty well as he liked. On this particular night the festivities had been more than usually prolonged, for as near as I could judge by the daylight which was creeping in through my window, it was about four o'clock in the morning when the big steel-sheeted door was opened and Salvolio came in, more than a little drunk. He brought with him, as I judged, one of his dancing girls, who apparently was privileged to see the sights of the palace.

"For a long time he stood in the doorway talking incoherently in a language which I think must have been Turkish, for I caught one or two words.

"Whoever the girl was, she seemed a little frightened. I could see that, because she shrank back from him, though his arm was about her shoulders and he was half supporting his weight upon her. There was fear, not only in the curious little glances she shot at me from time to time, but also in the averted face. Her story I was to learn. She was not of the class from whence Salvolio found the dancers who from time to time came up to the palace for his amusement and the amusement of his guests. She was the daughter of a Turkish merchant of Scutari, who had been received into the Catholic Church.

163

"Her father had gone down to Durazzo during the first Balkan war, and then Salvolio had seen the girl unknown to her parent, and there had been some rough kind of courtship, which ended in her running away on this very day and joining her ill-favoured lover at the palazzo. I tell you this because the fact had some bearing on my own fate.

"As I say, the girl was frightened and made as though to go from the dungeon. She was probably scared both by the unkempt prisoner and by the drunken man at her side. He, however, could not leave without showing to her something of his authority. He came lurching over near where I lay, his long knife balanced in his hand ready for emergencies, and broke into a string of vituperations of the character to which I was quite hardened.

"Then he took a flying kick at me and got home in my ribs, but again I experienced neither a sense of indignity nor any great hurt. Salvolio had treated me like this before, and I had survived it. In the midst of the tirade, looking past him, I was a new witness to an extraordinary scene.

"The girl stood in the open doorway, shrinking back against the door, looking with distress and pity at the spectacle which Salvolio's brutality afforded. Then suddenly there appeared beside her a tall Turk. He was grey-bearded and forbidding. She looked round and saw him, and her mouth opened to utter a cry, but with a gesture he silenced her, and pointed to the darkness outside.

"Without a word she cringed past him, her sandalled feet making no noise. All this time Salvolio was continuing his stream of abuse, but he must have seen the wonder in my eyes, for he stopped and turned.

"The old Turk took one stride forward, encircled his body with his left arm, and there they stood grotesquely like a couple who were going to start a waltz. The Turk was a head taller than Salvolio, and, as I could see, a man of immense strength.

"They looked at one another face to face, Salvolio rapidly recovering his senses...and then the Turk gave him a gentle punch in the ribs. That is what it seemed like to me, but Salvolio coughed horribly, went limp in the other's arms, and dropped with a thud to the ground. The Turk leant down soberly and wiped his long knife on the other's jacket before he put it back in the sash at his waist.

"Then with a glance at me be turned to go, but stopped at the door and looked back thoughtfully. He said something in Turkish which I could not understand, then he spoke in French.

" 'Who are you?' he asked.

"In as few words as possible I explained. He came over and looked at the manacle about my leg and shook his head.

"'You will never be able to get that undone,' he said.

"He caught hold of the chain, which was a fairly long one, bound it twice round his arm, and steadying his arm across his thigh, he turned with a sudden jerk. There was a smart 'snap' as the chain parted. He caught me by the shoulder and pulled me to my feet.

" 'Put the chain about your waist, Effendi,' he said, and he took a revolver from his belt and handed it to me.

" 'You may need this before we get back to Durazzo,' he said. His belt was literally bristling with weapons – I saw three revolvers besides the one I possessed – and he had evidently come prepared for trouble. We made our way from the dungeon into the clean-smelling world without.

"It was the second time I had been in the open air for eighteen months, and my knees were trembling under me with weakness and excitement. The old man shut the prison door behind us and walked on until we came up to the girl waiting for us by the lake side. She was weeping softly, and he spoke to her a few words in a low voice and her weeping ceased.

" 'This daughter of mine will show us the way,' he said, 'I do not know this part of the country – she knows it too well.'

"To cut a long story short," said Lexman, "we reached Durazzo in the afternoon. There was no attempt made to follow us up, and neither my absence nor the body of Salvolio was discovered until late in the afternoon. You must remember that nobody but Salvolio was allowed into my prison, and therefore nobody had the courage to make any investigations.

"The old man got me to his house without being observed, and brought a brother-in-law or some relative of his to remove the anklet. The name of my host was Hussein Effendi.

"That same night we left with a little caravan to visit some of the old man's relatives. He was not certain what would be the consequences of his act, and for safety's sake took this trip, which would enable him if needs be to seek sanctuary with some of the wilder Turkish tribes who would give him protection.

"In that three months I saw Albania as it is – it was an experience never to be forgotten!

"If there is a better man in God's world than Hiabam Hussein Effendi I have yet to meet him. It was he who provided me with money to leave Albania. I begged from him, too, the knife with which he had killed Salvolio. He had discovered that Kara was in England, and told me something of the Greek's occupation, which I had not known before. I crossed to Italy and went on to Milan. There it was that I learnt that an eccentric Englishman who had arrived a few days previously on one of the South American boats at Genoa, was in my hotel desperately ill.

"My hotel, I need hardly tell you, was not a very expensive one, and we were evidently the only two Englishmen in the place. I could do no less than go up and see what I could do for the poor fellow, who was pretty well gone when I saw him. I seemed to remember having seen him before, and when, looking round for some identification, I discovered his name, I readily recalled the circumstance.

"It was George Gathercole, who had returned from South America. He was suffering from malarial fever and blood poisoning, and for a week with an Italian doctor I fought as hard as any man could fight for his life. He was a trying patient," John Lexman smiled suddenly at the recollection, "vitriolic in his language, impatient and imperious in his attitude to his friends. He was, for example, terribly sensitive about his lost arm, and would not allow either the doctor or myself to enter the room until he was covered to the neck, nor would he eat or drink in our presence. Yet he was the bravest of the brave, careless of himself, and only fretful because he had not time to finish his new book. His indomitable spirit did not save him. He died on the 17th January of this year. I was in Genoa at the time, having gone there at his request to salve his belongings. When I returned he had been buried. I went through his papers, and it was then that I conceived my idea of how I might approach Kara.

"I found a letter from the Greek which had been addressed to Buenos Ayres, to await arrival, and then I remembered in a flash how Kara had told me he had sent George Gathercole to South America to report upon possible gold formations. I was determined to kill Kara, and determined to kill him in such a way that I myself would cover every trace of my complicity.

"Even as he had planned my downfall, scheming every step and covering his trail, so did I plan, to bring about his death that no suspicion should fall on me.

"I knew his house. I knew something of his habits. I knew the fear in which he went when he was in England and away from the feudal guards who had surrounded him in Albania. I knew of his famous door with its steel latch, and I was planning to circumvent all these precautions and bring to him not only the death he deserved, but a full knowledge of his fate before he died.

"Gathercole had some money, about £140. I took £100 of this for my own use, knowing that I should have sufficient in London to recompense his heirs, and the remainder of the money with all such documents he had, save those which identified him with Kara, I handed over to the British Consul.

"I was not unlike the dead man. My beard had grown wild and I knew enough of Gathercole's eccentricities to live the part. The first step I took was to announce my arrival by inference. I am a fairly good journalist with a wide general knowledge, and with this, corrected by reference to the necessary books which I found in the British Museum library, I was able to turn out a very respectable article on Patagonia.

"This I sent to *The Times* with one of Gathercole's cards, and, as you know, it was printed. My next step was to find suitable lodgings between Chelsea and Scotland Yard. I was fortunate in being able to hire a furnished flat, the owner of which was going to the south of France for three months. I paid the rent in advance, and since I dropped all the eccentricities I had assumed to support the character of Gathercole, I must have impressed the owner, who took me without references.

"I had several suits of new clothes made, not in London," he smiled, "but in Manchester, and again I made myself as trim as possible to avoid after-identification. When I had got these together in my flat I chose my day. In the morning I sent two trunks with most of my personal belongings to the Great Midland Hotel.

"In the afternoon I went to Cadogan Square and hung about until I saw Kara drive off. It was my first view of him since I had left Albania, and it required all my self-control to prevent me springing at him in the street and tearing at him with my hands.

"Once he was out of sight I went to the house, adopting all the style and all the mannerisms of poor Gathercole. My beginning was unfortunate, for, with a shock, I recognised in the valet a fellow-convict who had been with me in the warder's cottage on the morning of my escape from Dartmoor. There was no mistaking him, and when I heard his voice I was certain. Would he recognise me, I wondered, in spite of my beard and my eye-glasses?

"Apparently he did not. I gave him every chance. I thrust my face into his, and on my second visit challenged him, in the eccentric way which poor old Gathercole had, to test the grey of my beard. For the moment, however, I was satisfied with my brief experiment, and after a reasonable interval I went away, returning to my place off Victoria Street and waiting till the evening.

"In my observation of the house, whilst I was waiting for Kara to depart, I had noticed that there were two distinct telephone wires running down to the roof. I guessed, rather than knew, that one of these telephones was a private wire, and knowing something of Kara's fear I presumed that that wire would lead to a police office, or at any rate to a guardian of some kind or other. Kara had the same arrangement in Albania, connecting the palazzo with the gendarme posts at Alesso. This much Hussein told me.

"That night I made a reconnaissance of the house and saw Kara's window was lit, and at ten minutes past ten I rang the bell, and I think it was then that I applied the test of the beard. Kara was in his room, the valet told me, and led the way upstairs. I had come prepared to deal with this valet, for I had had an especial reason for wishing that he should not be interrogated by the police. On a plain card I had written the number he bore in Dartmoor, and had added the words, 'I know you, get out of here quick.'

"As he turned to lead the way upstairs I flung the envelope containing the card on the table in the hall. In an inside pocket as near to my body as I could put them I had the two candles. How I should use them both I had already decided. The valet ushered me into Kara's room, and once more I stood in the presence of the man who had killed my girl and blotted out all that was beautiful in life for me."

There was a breathless silence when he paused. TX leant back in his chair, his head upon his breast, his arms folded, his eyes watching the other intently.

The Chief Commissioner, with a heavy frown and pursed lips, sat stroking his moustache and looking under his shaggy eyebrows at the speaker. The French police officer, his hands thrust deep in his pockets, his head on one side, was taking in every word eagerly. The sallow-faced Russian, impassive of face, might have been a carved ivory mask. O'Grady, the American, the stump of a dead cigar between his teeth, shifted impatiently with every pause as though he would hurry forward the denouement.

Presently John Lexman went on.

"He slipped from the bed and came across to meet me as I closed the door behind me.

" 'Ah, Mr Gathercole,' he said in that silky tone of his, and held out his hand.

"I did not speak. I just looked at him with a sort of fierce joy in my heart the like of which I had never before experienced.

"And then he saw in my eyes the truth and half reached for the telephone.

"But at that moment I was on him. He was a child in my hands. All the bitter anguish he had brought upon me, all the hardships of starved days and freezing nights had strengthened and hardened me. I had come back to London disguised with a false arm, and this I shook free. It was merely a gauntlet of thin wood which I had had made for me in Paris.

"I flung him back on the bed and half knelt, half laid on him.

" 'Kara,' I said, 'you are going to die, a more merciful death than my wife died.'

"He tried to speak. His soft hands gesticulated wildly, but I was half lying on one arm and held the other.

"I whispered in his ear: 'Nobody will know who killed you, Kara, think of that! I shall go scot free – and you will be the centre of a fine mystery! All your letters will be read, all your life will be examined and the world will know you – for what you are!'

"I released his arm for just as long as it took to draw my knife and strike. I think he died instantly," John Lexman said simply.

"I left him where he was and went to the door. I had not much time to spare. I took the candles from my pocket. They were already ductile from the heat of my body.

"I lifted up the steel latch of the door and propped up the latch with the smaller of the two candles, one end of which was on the middle socket and the other beneath the latch. The heat of the room, I knew, would still further soften the candle and let the latch down in a short time.

"I was prepared for the telephone by his bedside, though I did not know whither it led. The presence of the paper-knife decided me. I balanced it across the silver cigarette box so that one end came under the telephone receiver; under the other end I put the second candle, which I had to cut to fit. On top of the paper-knife at the candle end I balanced the only two books I could find in the room, and fortunately they were heavy.

"I had no means of knowing how long it would take to melt the candle to a state of flexion which would allow the full weight of the books to bear upon the candle end of the paperknife and fling off the receiver. I was hoping that Fisher had taken my warning and had gone. When I opened the door softly I heard his footsteps in the hall below. There was nothing to do but to finish the play.

"I turned and addressed an imaginary conversation to Kara. It was horrible, but there was something about it which aroused in me a curious sense of humour, and I wanted to laugh and laugh and laugh!

"I heard the man coming up the stairs and closed the door gingerly. What length of time would it take for the candle to bend?

"To establish the *alibi* completely I determined to hold Fisher in conversation, and this was all the easier since apparently he had not seen the envelope I had left on the table downstairs. I had not long to wait, for suddenly with a crash I heard the steel latch fall in its place. Under the effect of the heat the candle had bent sooner than I had expected. I asked Fisher what was the meaning of the sound and he explained. I passed down the stairs talking all the time. I found a cab at Sloane Square and drove to my lodgings. Underneath my overcoat I was partly dressed in evening kit.

"Ten minutes after I entered the door of my flat I came out a beardless man about town, not to be distinguished from the thousand others who would be found that night walking the promenade of any of the great music-halls. From Victoria Street I drove straight to Scotland Yard. It was no more than a coincidence that whilst I should have been speaking with you all, the second candle should have bent and the alarm be given in the very office in which I was sitting.

"I assure you all in all earnestness that I did not suspect the cause of that ringing until Mr Mansus spoke.

"There, gentlemen, is my story!" He threw out his arms.

"You may do with me as you will. Kara was a murderer, dyed a hundred times in innocent blood. I have done all that I set myself to do – that and no more – that and no less. I had thought to go away to America, but the nearer the day of my departure approached, the more vivid came the memory of the plans which she and I had formed, my girl...my poor martyred girl!"

He sat at the little table, his hands clasped before him, his face lined and white.

"And that is the end!" he said suddenly with a wry smile.

"Not quite!"

TX swung round with a gasp. It was Belinda Mary who spoke.

"I can carry it on," she said.

She was wonderfully self-possessed, thought TX, but then TX never thought anything of her but that she was "wonderfully" something or the other.

"Most of your story is true, Mr Lexman," said this amazing girl, oblivious of the amazed eyes that were staring at her, "but Kara deceived you in one respect."

"What do you mean?" asked John Lexman, rising unsteadily to his feet.

For answer she rose and walked back to the door with the chintz curtains and flung it open. There was a wait which seemed an eternity, and then through the doorway came a girl, slim and grave and beautiful.

"My God!" whispered TX, "Grace Lexman!"

23

They went out and left them alone, two people who found in this moment a heaven which is not beyond the reach of humanity, but which is seldom attained to. Belinda Mary had an eager audience all to her very self.

"Of course she didn't die," she said scornfully. "Kara was playing on his fears all the time. He never even harmed her – in the way Mr Lexman feared. He told Mrs Lexman that her husband was dead, just as he told John Lexman his wife was gone. What happened was that he brought her back to England – "

"Who?" asked TX incredulously.

"Grace Lexman," said the girl with a smile. "You wouldn't think it possible, but when you realise that he had a yacht of his own, and that he could travel up from whatever landing place he chose to his house in Cadogan Square by motor car, and that he could take her straight away into his cellar without disturbing his household, you'll understand that the only difficulty he had was in landing her. It was in the lower cellar that I found her."

"You found her in the cellar?" demanded the Chief Commissioner.

The girl nodded.

"I found her and the dog – you heard how Kara terrified her – and I killed the dog with my own hands," she said a little proudly, and then shivered; "it was very beastly," she admitted.

"And she's been living with you all this time and you've said nothing?" asked TX incredulously.

Belinda Mary nodded.

"And that is why you didn't want me to know where you were living?"

She nodded again.

"You see, she was very ill," she said, "and I had to nurse her up; and, of course, I knew that it was Lexman who had killed Kara, and I couldn't tell you about Grace Lexman without betraying him. So when Mr Lexman decided to tell his story I thought I'd better supply the grand denouement."

The men looked at one another.

"What are we going to do about Lexman?" asked the Chief Commissioner, "and by the way, TX, how does all this fit your theories?"

"Fairly well," replied TX coolly; "obviously, the man who committed the murder was the man introduced into the room as Gathercole, and as obviously it was not Gathercole, although to all appearance he had lost his left arm."

"Why obviously?" asked the Chief Commissioner.

"Because," answered TX Meredith, "the real Gathercole had lost his *right arm* – that was the one error Lexman made."

"H'm," the Chief pulled at his moustache and looked inquiringly round the room, "we have to make up our minds very quickly about Lexman," he said. "What do you think, Carlneau?"

The Frenchman shrugged his shoulders.

"For my part I should not only importune your Home Secretary to pardon him, but I should recommend him for a pension," he said flippantly.

"What do you think, Savorsky?"

The Russian smiled a little.

"It is a very impressing story," he said dispassionately; "it occurs to me that if you intend bringing your M. Lexman to judgment you are likely to expose some very pretty scandals. Incidentally," he said, stroking his trim little moustache, "I might remark that any exposure which drew attention to the lawless conditions of Albania would not be regarded by my Government with favour."

The Chief Commissioner's eyes twinkled and he nodded.

"That is also my view," said the Chief of the Italian bureau; "naturally we are greatly interested in all that happens on the Adriatic littoral. It seems to me that Kara has come to a very merciful end, and I am not inclined to regard a prosecution of Mr Lexman with equanimity."

"Well, I guess the political aspect of the case doesn't affect us very much," said O'Grady; "but as one who was once mighty near asphyxiated by stirring up the wrong kind of mud, I should leave the matter where it is."

The Chief Commissioner was deep in thought, and Belinda Mary eyed him anxiously.

"Tell him to come in," he said bluntly.

The girl went and brought John Lexman and his wife, and they came in hand in hand, supremely and serenely happy whatever the future might hold for them. The Chief Commissioner cleared his throat.

"Lexman, we're all very much obliged to you," he said, "for a very interesting story and a most interesting theory. What you have done, as I understand the matter," he proceeded deliberately, "is to put yourself in the murderer's place and advance a theory not only as to how the murder was actually committed, but as to the motive for that murder. It is, I might say, a remarkable piece of reconstruction." He spoke very deliberately and swept away John Lexman's astonished interruption with a stern hand. "Please wait, and do not speak until I am out of hearing," he growled. "You have got into the skin of the actual assassin and have spoken most convincingly. One might almost think that the man who killed Remington Kara was actually standing before us. For that piece of impersonation we are all very grateful." He glared round over his spectacles at his understanding colleagues and they murmured approvingly.

He looked at his watch.

"Now, I'm afraid I must be off." He crossed the room and put out his hand to John Lexman. "I wish you good luck," he said, and took both Grace Lexman's hands in his. "One of these days," he said paternally, "I shall come down to Beston Tracey, and your husband shall tell me another and a happier story."

He paused at the door as he was going out and, looking back, caught the grateful eyes of Lexman.

"By the way, Mr Lexman," he said hesitatingly, "I don't think I should ever write a story called 'The Clue of the Twisted Candle' if I were you."

John Lexman shook his head.

"It will never be written," he said, " – by me."

Edgar Wallace

Big Foot

Footprints and a dead woman bring together Superintendent Minton
and the amateur sleuth Mr Cardew. Who is the man in the shrubbery?
Who is the singer of the haunting Moorish tune? Why is Hannah
Shaw so determined to go to Pawsy, 'a dog lonely place' she had
previously detested? Death lurks in the dark and someone must solve
the mystery before BIG FOOT strikes again, in a yet more fiendish
manner.

Bones In London

The new Managing Director of Schemes Ltd has an elegant London
office and a theatrically dressed assistant – however, Bones, as he is
better known, is bored. Luckily there is a slump in the shipping
market and it is not long before Joe and Fred Pole pay Bones a visit.
They are totally unprepared for Bones' unnerving style of doing
business, unprepared for his unique style of innocent and endearing
mischief.

Edgar Wallace

Bones of the River

'Taking the little paper from the pigeon's leg, Hamilton saw it was from Sanders and marked URGENT. *Send Bones instantly to Lujamalababa… Arrest and bring to headquarters the witch doctor.*'

It is a time when the world's most powerful nations are vying for colonial honour, a time of trading steamers and tribal chiefs. In the mysterious African territories administered by Commissioner Sanders, Bones persistently manages to create his own unique style of innocent and endearing mischief.

The Daffodil Mystery

When Mr Thomas Lyne, poet, poseur and owner of Lyne's Emporium insults a cashier, Odette Rider, she resigns. Having summoned detective Jack Tarling to investigate another employee, Mr Milburgh, Lyne now changes his plans. Tarling and his Chinese companion refuse to become involved. They pay a visit to Odette's flat and in the hall Tarling meets Sam, convicted felon and protégé of Lyne. Next morning Tarling discovers a body. The hands are crossed on the breast, adorned with a handful of daffodils.

Edgar Wallace

The Joker
(USA: The Colossus)

While the millionaire Stratford Harlow is in Princetown, not only does he meet with his lawyer Mr Ellenbury but he gets his first glimpse of the beautiful Aileen Rivers, niece of the actor and convicted felon Arthur Ingle. When Aileen is involved in a car accident on the Thames Embankment, the driver is James Carlton of Scotland Yard. Later that evening Carlton gets a call. It is Aileen. She needs help.

The Square Emerald
(USA: The Girl From Scotland Yard)

'Suicide on the left,' says Chief Inspector Coldwell pleasantly, as he and Leslie Maughan stride along the Thames Embankment during a brutally cold night. A gaunt figure is sprawled across the parapet. But Coldwell soon discovers that Peter Dawlish, fresh out of prison for forgery, is not considering suicide but murder. Coldwell suspects Druze as the intended victim. Maughan disagrees. If Druze dies, she says, 'It will be because he does not love children!'